# MARCUS MAKES IT BIG

# ALSO BY KEVIN HART

*Marcus Makes a Movie*

# MARCUS
## MAKES IT BIG

# KEVIN HART
WITH **GEOFF RODKEY**

ILLUSTRATED BY **DAVID COOPER**

CROWN BOOKS FOR YOUNG READERS ♛ NEW YORK

All rights reserved. Published in the United States by
Crown Books for Young Readers, an imprint of Random House Children's Books,
a division of Penguin Random House LLC, New York.

Crown and the colophon are registered trademarks of
Penguin Random House LLC.

Visit us on the Web! rhcbooks.com

Educators and librarians, for a variety of teaching tools, visit us at
RHTeachersLibrarians.com

Library of Congress Cataloging-in-Publication Data is available upon request.
ISBN 978-0-593-17918-5 (hardcover)
ISBN 978-0-593-17920-8 (ebook)

The text of this book is set in 12-point Kievit Slab Pro.
Interior design by Carol Ly

Printed in the United States of America
10 9 8 7 6 5 4 3 2 1
First Edition

To my kids, Kaori, Kenzo, Hendrix, and Heaven.
And your whole generation of future groundbreakers.
Don't stress over clicks, likes, or page views!
Just do the hard work to create awesome stuff
that makes you proud.
And you can change the world!

# CHAPTER 1

# THERE IS A LIMO
# IN FRONT OF MY BUILDING!

I could NOT believe it.

There was a limo driving up our street!

A LIM-O-ZINE! A stretch!

A long, black, movie-star-carrying kind of ride.

It wasn't there for the reason you'd think. It wasn't 'cause some rich dude took the wrong exit off the expressway. Or a bunch of high school kids chipped in to rent one for prom.

It wasn't even Prom Night! It was seven in the morning! On a Tuesday!

And this is the wild thing: that limo was coming FOR ME!

It was picking ME up!

(Plus my dad. But he was just along for the ride.)

Now, I bet you're thinking: the day a real-life limo pulls up outside your door? To take you someplace important enough to send a LIMO?

That must be the greatest day of your life!

Right?

And in some ways it was.

A whole lot of amazing stuff was happening to me.

But by the time that limo pulled up in front of our building, I wasn't feeling too amazing.

Fact: I felt like the Swamp Zombie.

You know that comic? About the dude who turned into a plant? Wasn't even human anymore? Just a big nasty blob of slimy leaves and rotten old gunk?

That's how I was feeling when that limo rolled up.

Like a grimy, smelly Swamp Zombie.

Head spinning. Guts churning. With actual stink on me.

Driver dude got out of the front seat. Came around to open the door for me and Dad. Just like in the movies.

Dad gave him a big smile. Said, "Thank you, sir!"

Driver dude smiled back. Gave Dad a nod. Said, "Yessir! Welcome aboard!"

Then they both looked at me like, *Get on in there!*

Before I climbed in, I said a little prayer.

This is what it was:

*Lord, please don't let me barf in this limo.*

It wasn't a joke. I was feeling about ninety percent guaranteed to toss my breakfast all over the back of that stretch.

And the reason I was such a mess . . .

See, what had happened was . . .

Aw, man! I started this story in the wrong place.

Let me back up.

## CHAPTER 2

# THE WORLD'S GREATEST SUPERHERO

First time I ever drew a Toothpick comic, I was nine years old. My mom had this real bad cancer. It was eating her up inside. And I just wanted to . . . GRRRRRR! Beat that cancer down, man! Save my mama like a superhero!

But I couldn't. I was just a little kid. Doctors couldn't even save her.

That cancer was like a supervillain. THE DOOM. Death itself. Nothing could stop it!

Except for Toothpick.

He was a superhero. Looked kinda like me, all skinny and whatnot. Except taller. And STRONG. Had these finger spears. Six-inch razors coming out of every nail on his hand. He'd use them to SQUICK-SQUICK! Slice up the Doom like deli meat!

Save my mama! Save the world!

None of it was real. Toothpick was just a comic I made up. But drawing him made me feel better.

After Mom passed, I kept drawing. For three years, I drew Toothpick comics almost every day. Pretty soon, he wasn't just fighting the Doom. He took on a whole mess of bad guys. Dead Eye, Doctor Mindsuck, Purple Witch ... Toothpick showed them all who's boss!

And after three years of drawing every day, I was getting good at it. I figured it was just a matter of time before Capital Comics gave me a twelve-issue run! Put me on the road to making Toothpick the greatest superhero in the history of comics!

Bigger than Batguy! Bigger than Superguy! Kind of hero you see on T-shirts! Roller coasters! Underwear!

And MOVIES.

Back then, I used to think if I wanted to get a Toothpick movie made, I'd have to put out a bunch of Toothpick comics first. Make those a hit. Then do a movie afterward.

I never once thought, *What if I just straight-up make a Toothpick movie NOW?*

I figured you needed a zillion dollars and a whole lot of special equipment to even TRY to make a movie.

But then I got stuck in this after-school film class. And I met Sierra.

Here's the thing about Sierra: she is ANNOYING. She's a year older than me. About a foot taller. And the girl thinks she's all that.

But here's the other thing about Sierra: When it comes

to making movies? She actually IS all that! As good as I am at drawing comics? She's even better at making movies.

Plus, she's got hustle. Which you need if you want to make a movie. It's hard work! I could write a whole book about how hard it is to make a movie!

Actually, I did. It's called *Marcus Makes a Movie*. You might want to check it out.

But let me spoil the ending for you: we made a movie!

*Toothpick Fights the Doom!* The dopest fourteen minutes and thirty-six seconds ever!

It wasn't just me. It took a whole team.

I wrote the script. Then I rewrote it about fifty times, till Sierra said it was good to go. When we shot it, I played Toothpick, plus Marko Jackson—that's the regular kid who turns into Toothpick whenever he puts this magic toothpick in his mouth.

Sierra directed the whole thing. She also played Toothpick's sidekick, Genie.

We got big bully Tyrell from the neighborhood to play the Doom. Tyrell looks scary just walking down the street, so he made a dope supervillain.

Tyrell's real-life crew—Sly, Naz, and Double D—they played the Doom's henchmen.

Pretty Jazmin from film class played Angel, the girl Toothpick saves.

We got my boy, Khalid, to run the camera for us. Even though sometimes the camera was just Sierra's phone.

Amari laid down a soundtrack for us, 'cause he's a dope musician.

It took A LOT of us to make that movie. Lots of people. Lots of time. Lots of work. And lots of fights. Especially between me and Sierra. 'Cause that girl has opinions! And so do I.

Whole thing felt like pushing a big rock up an even bigger mountain. There were times I didn't think we'd ever get it done.

But we did. And when we finished? *Toothpick Fights the Doom!* was AWESOME. Funny and scary, but mostly funny. 'Cause scrawny little me dressed up in a superhero costume, beating down big Tyrell? Man, that can't be anything BUT funny.

I dedicated the whole movie to my mama, God rest her soul. 'Cause she loved to laugh.

I was SO PROUD of that movie! There's nothing in the world like the feeling I got from making it. I dreamed up something in my mind that never existed before. Then my friends and I brought it to life!

It went from being just a story in my head to a REAL THING that other folks could have fun watching!

We put it up on MeTube. And at first, nobody but us watched it. We tried tagging a bunch of celebrities and movie stars like Tevin Bart. Asked them to check it out, maybe share it on social. None of them did. So the page views were just sad. After it had been up a month, we barely had three hundred views! And most of those were just us, watching it over and over again.

Every day, I'd go online and check that number. Some days, it wouldn't go up at all.

I'd check it on Thursday: *302 views.*

Check it again Friday: *302 views.* Again!

It was like watching paint dry!

But it didn't matter. My dad got us a room down at the community center, and we put on a screening there one Saturday night. Everybody who worked on the movie came, plus all our friends and families. And they loved it! We watched it twice, eating popcorn and drinking soda together.

We had so much fun! It was the best night of my life!

I went to bed that Saturday SO HAPPY about what we made. I was hyped to create more new stuff—draw a bunch of fresh Toothpick comics, maybe even make a whole other movie someday!

But I figured the story of *Toothpick Fights the Doom!* was over.

Then I woke up Sunday morning with Sierra screaming in my ear through the phone.

Tevin Bart had shared the link on social after all! Then a whole bunch of other folks shared it, too!

Our movie was going viral!

A quarter million views!

Going up by thousands of views a minute!

And that's where THIS story starts.

# CHAPTER 3

# I'M FAMOUS!

"OH MAN OH MAN!"

I couldn't believe it. Every time I hit refresh on my *Toothpick Fights the Doom!* MeTube page, the counter jumped by another couple thousand:

*251,132 . . .*

*253,564 . . .*

People all over the world must've been watching it!

"THIS IS CRAZY!" I was so hyped, I almost knocked Dad's laptop off our living room couch.

"Quit yelling in my ear!" Sierra shouted through the phone.

"Quit yelling in MY ear!" I shouted right back.

She kept on shouting. "IT'S SO AMAZING!"

I did, too. "AAAAAAAH!"

Dad came in from the bathroom, wearing boxers and an undershirt. Still holding the towel from his shower.

"Marcus! Settle down! It's Sunday morning! You gonna wake the whole building up!"

"Dad! *Toothpick* went viral! Got a quarter million views!"

"What now?"

"Tevin Bart shared it on social! Bunch of other folks did, too! I'M FAMOUS!"

Dad stepped past me, smelling of body wash. He looked at the laptop to check the page views for himself.

"Daaaaaaang . . . ! That number's real?"

"Yeah, Dad! It's real!"

"So what'd Tevin Bart do? He put it on Flitter? Did he flit about it?"

"No, he shared it on ClickChat. Or maybe both! I dunno."

"DOPE!" Dad straightened up. Gave me a smile so big it took up half his face. "You did it, son!" Then he squeezed me in a bear hug.

"AAAH! Watch the phone, Dad!"

"Who you on with?" he asked me.

"Sierra."

"Morning, Mr. Jenkins!" Sierra called out, loud enough for him to hear through the phone.

"Congratulations, girl!" he told her. "You on your way to the Oscars! Gonna be Best Director someday!"

"Thank you, Mr. Jenkins!"

Dad gave me a friendly poke in the belly. "What'd I tell you? That movie was TOO GOOD not to get some eyes on it." Then he checked the time on the cable box. "Ooop! I gotta get to work." He headed for his bedroom to get dressed.

"I can't believe this," Sierra was saying. "I! Can! Not! Believe it!"

I sat down on the couch and hit refresh again.

*260,906 . . .*

"This is nuts," I said. "It's just nuts."

I opened up Tevin Bart's ClickChat page to see for myself what he'd posted.

There it was, right at the top of his feed: a screen grab of me in my Toothpick costume, doing a karate kick off a playground slide at big Tyrell. Tyrell was dressed as the Doom in his Grim Reaper outfit, looking all shocked that little me was beating him down.

Under the screen grab was a link to the MeTube page, plus Tevin Bart's comment:

I couldn't believe it, man! Tevin Bart was talking about us! WE were the "these kids" kids!

I checked the page views again.

*272,120 . . .*

Shooting up like a rocket! This was the greatest day of my life!

And somebody was yelling in my ear.

It was Sierra. I'd forgotten I was even holding the phone.

"OKAY?" she was saying.

"Okay what?" I asked her.

She huffed out a big sigh. "Marcus, did you hear a word I've been saying?"

"No."

She gave me another big sigh. But I was just being honest.

"This is our shot!" she told me. "If we play this right, we can build something BIG. We could be STARS. But we gotta make a PLAN. And get on it FAST. You feel me?"

It was just like Sierra. Always thinking three steps ahead.

"Heck, yeah!" I told her. "We should make a sequel!"

"For certain!" she said. "But right now, I gotta go to

church. I'm leaving my phone at home. Not gonna be reachable till later. So don't do anything stupid while I'm gone. Okay?"

That got me mad. "What would I even do that's stupid?" I asked.

"I'm juuust saaaying," she said in her schoolteacher voice. "Sometimes your mouth gets ahead of your brain."

She wasn't wrong. But I didn't want to hear that. I was flying too high!

"Don't even start," I told her. "I'll talk to you later."

After we got off the phone, I hit the refresh button again.

*280,620 . . .*

Man! It was blowing up!

Dad came back into the room. He was wearing his work uniform.

"You getting on that laundry?" he asked.

"What now?"

"Sunday morning, son! Gotta get it in before Miss Kayla wakes up."

My best friend, J.R., lives in the apartment downstairs. Miss Kayla's his mom. And there's just one laundry machine in the basement for all three units: them, us, and old Mr. Hampton up on the top floor.

When Dad works a Sunday shift, it's my job to do the laundry. If I start it too late, I run into J.R.'s mom. 'Cause she also does their laundry on Sundays.

Fact: J.R.'s mom is a laundry room nightmare. She'll do

like ten loads in a row, and she won't share. So if I don't get mine done before she comes down and starts hogging the machine? It's gonna be a very long day in that laundry room.

So the smart move is to get it in early, before she even wakes up.

But I wasn't feeling it that morning. How could I wash clothes on the greatest day of my life?

"Do I really gotta do the laundry?" I asked Dad.

"Why wouldn't you?" he asked right back.

"'Cause my movie's going viral!"

"What's that got to do with laundry?"

"Dad! I'm FAMOUS!"

He gave me a look like, *Puh-leeeze.* "You think famous people don't need clean drawers? Think Tevin Bart doesn't have to do HIS laundry?"

"I bet he doesn't!"

"Well, you're not Tevin Bart yet, son. So get that laundry going before Miss Kayla makes it hard on you. And don't forget to wash your good shirt."

My good shirt was on the floor of my bedroom, 'cause I'd worn it to the movie party the night before. I went and got it, along with the rest of the dirty clothes in my laundry sack. I was getting Dad's laundry when I heard him open the front door to leave.

"Love you, son! Congrats again on those page views!"

"Thanks, Dad! Love you, too!"

"Don't let that good shirt go in the dryer! Put it on a hanger to line dry. And I'm picking up burgers for dinner. Text me your order!"

"I got you!" I told him.

Then he was gone. A minute later, I followed him out, heading for the basement with our laundry. Before I left, I stopped to check the page views again.

*312,774 . . .*

Man! I couldn't believe I had to do laundry on the same day I went viral.

There were two loads' worth of clothes. After I got the first one in, I went back upstairs. Made myself a bowl of cereal. Ate it up. Then I checked the numbers again.

*407,330 . . .*

ZAAP!

Seeing that number jump by a whole hundred thousand was like an electric shock to my brain!

I felt like ELEKTRO!

You know that dude? From the comic books? Elektro's a supervillain. Feeds on electricity. He's like an energy vampire. Addicted to it! Gotta keep sucking up those volts, or he gets weak. Loses his power.

That's how it felt with me and those page views. When I saw that big jump, I was like, "YAAAAAAS!"

But when I refreshed it again, a minute later? And the number only went up by a thousand or so? It was almost a letdown.

Getting all those page views just made me want MORE of them. Like I was a vampire, but for clicks!

I figured if I didn't check it for a while, the number would go up more. Then when I rechecked it, I'd get a bigger jolt. So I closed up the laptop. Called J.R. downstairs to see if he wanted to hang.

"I'M FAMOUS!" I yelled when he picked up his cell. Then I told him what was up.

He sounded happy for me. But not THAT happy.

"You want to come upstairs, play some GameBox?" I asked him.

"No, man," he said. "I'm on the bus already. Got a basketball game across town."

"Oh. Well, hit me up when you get back."

"Aaaite."

After I hung up the phone, I didn't know what to do with myself.

It was too soon to go downstairs and swap the laundry.

I had math homework. But I don't like doing homework even when I'm NOT going viral.

I got my comics stuff out to make a new Toothpick. Figured I should come up with a story for the movie sequel.

I drew Toothpick shooting up through the sky into outer space. 'Cause that's how I felt. Blasting off like a rocket!

But I couldn't make myself sit still long enough to draw more than just one panel.

All I wanted to do was check those page views again. I was itching for them!

I went back to Dad's laptop.

*450,224 . . .*

ZAP! Another Elektro jolt!

Every single one of those views was a person! Watching MY movie!

I was FAMOUS!

My whole life had changed! It must have!

Except when I looked around, it seemed like NOTHING had changed.

Same old tiny apartment. Nobody in it but me.

Just another lonely Sunday. Dad off at work. Me just sitting there.

What was I supposed to do? Keep staring at those numbers all day?

I felt like I should be with people. Celebrating! Or something.

That's why I started the group text.

## CHAPTER 4

# I PROBABLY SHOULD NOT HAVE STARTED THAT GROUP TEXT

But I did.

I tagged in all the kids who'd worked on *Toothpick Fights the Doom!* Except for Sierra, 'cause she was at church.

I hit up big scary Tyrell, who played the Doom.

Pretty Jazmin, who played the girl I saved from the Doom.

Amari, who laid down the dope tunes for the soundtrack.

And quiet Khalid, who ran the camera for us.

Shot off three quick texts to them:

WE WENT VIRAL!!!!

TEVIN BART SHARED US ON CLICKCHAT!!!

450,000 VIEWS GOIN UP FAST!!!

Jazmin answered first:

I was feeling that emoji love!

For about three seconds.

Then it all went sideways. 'Cause the NEXT thing she texted was:

JAZMIN

> **OMG U HAVE TO LINK TO MY CHANNEL**

JAZMIN

> **LINK TO MY CHANNEL ON UR PAGE!!!**

See, Jazmin's got her own MeTube channel. She posts hair and makeup videos. They don't get much traffic. Like thirty views, tops.

But she cares A LOT about her channel.

And I didn't even really HAVE a channel. I mean, I did. But the only thing on it was the *Toothpick* movie. I barely even knew how MeTube channels worked!

So I was just trying to figure out how to even DO a link to her page when Jazmin texted again:

**HYPE ME IN A VLOG!!!!!!!**

I was staring at that text like, *Whaaat?* when she called me up and started yelling:

"You gotta vlog me, Marcus! Vlog me NOW!"

"What's that even mean?"

"Are you serious?"

"Yes! What's a vlog?"

"It's a video! Where you talk to the camera! You gotta post a—"

Then she got cut off. 'Cause my phone died.

It was out of charge already. See, my phone's a hundred years old. And it can't hold a charge any better than a hundred-year-old man can hold his pee.

By the time I got the charger from my bedroom, plugged my phone in behind the couch, and restarted it, I had seventeen new texts from Jazmin.

**ANSWER THE PHONE!**

**DON'T DUCK ME!**

**MARCUS!!!!!!!!!!**

**PICK UP!**

I called her back. "I ain't ducking you! My phone died!"

"Just listen to me!" she said. "You gotta shoot a vlog! Talk into the camera! Say, 'If you want your nails looking fierce like Toothpick, get yourself over to the *Jazmin Stylez* channel! Featuring Jazmin Baptiste, THE STAR OF THE MOVIE!'"

"I gotta say THAT?"

"YES! It's true, ain't it?"

It was maybe half true. Jazmin had done my nails up for the movie. Used some press-on acrylics to make it look like Toothpick had finger spears.

And she'd filmed me getting my Toothpick nails done. Three times! That's how many "how-to-do-your-nails" vids she had on her channel. Starring me! And I was not what you'd call proud of being the poster boy for nail extensions. That was just the price I had to pay to get Jazmin to do my Toothpick finger-spear nails.

But saying she was "THE STAR" of the movie? That wasn't close to true.

I mean, yeah. She played Angel. But Angel was, like, the fourth-biggest character. Out of five.

And real talk? Jazmin's acting game is NOT fierce. One thing that made *Toothpick Fights the Doom!* so funny? Was her trying to be all Serious Dramatic Actress-y . . . and just looking corny.

Now, had anybody ever told her that? No. We had not.

Was I going to start now? DEFINITELY NOT.

'Cause the girl is older than me. Probably stronger than me. And SUPER pretty. Like, off-the-charts pretty. So I have always been a little bit scared of Jazmin. And I just wanted to make her happy.

So I pretty much rolled over and did what she told me. Even though I did not exactly want to.

I shot a video. Told everybody if they wanted finger-spear-looking nails like Toothpick, they should head over to the *Jazmin Stylez* channel. Run by Jazmin Baptiste, ONE OF the stars of the movie.

I shot the whole thing in one take. And fact: it kinda looked trash. But I uploaded it to MeTube. Linked to her page. And it got her off my back. She texted me:

> **THANK UUUUUU!!**
> ♥♥♥♥♥♥

I was feeling good about those heart emojis.
I was also thinking, *Glad THAT'S over.*
But then Amari popped off in the group text:

AMARI

> **LINK TO MY CHANNEL TOO!!!**

AMARI

> **FINNA DROP A NEW TRACK!! HOOK ME UP WITH A SHOUT OUT!!!**

Amari ALSO had a MeTube channel, for his music videos. They were pretty dope. I was even in a couple of them.

And I couldn't post a vlog for Jazmin and then NOT hook up Amari.

So I shot another one. Hyped Amari's new track. Plus his old tracks. Plus his DJ business.

Then I uploaded that. So now my channel had THREE videos.

And I was thinking, *Okay, that is ENOUGH.*

But then Khalid jumped in the group text.

On top of doing the camera work and the special effects for my *Toothpick* movie, Khalid's big into this kind of animation called "stop-motion." So he texted:

KHALID

Can u post my stop motion

KHALID

I don't have a channel

KHALID

But I can send it to u

KHALID

> **Post it on ur page
> ok???????**

This whole situation was getting out of hand.

Khalid was my boy! I wanted to do right by him!

But I'd seen his stop-motion movie. And it was not what you'd call finished.

It was ten seconds long. Didn't have a story. Or sound. The lighting was shady. Animation was all jerky. It just wasn't DONE yet.

So I wasn't too hyped about putting it on my MeTube page.

But Khalid was my brethren! I didn't want to NOT help him. Especially when I'd just hooked up Jazmin and Amari.

So Khalid sent me his stop-motion movie. And I uploaded that, too.

By this point—I don't even know what time it was—*Toothpick* was still racking up those clicks. It was fixin' to blow past 700,000 views!

I was riding high! Sucking in that page view energy like Elektro!

Then big scary Tyrell threw down in the group text and tripped me out in a whole OTHER direction. Here's what he texted:

TYRELL

> **WE RICH Y'ALL**
> $ $ $ $ $ $ $

# CHAPTER 5

# I'M RICH!

It took my brain a second to puzzle out what Tyrell even meant.

Rich.

*Rich?*

RIIIICH!

"AAAAAAH!" I yelled so loud, old Mr. Hampton upstairs banged on the floor to shut me up.

My heart was beating like a drum. I texted everybody:

> **Can u for real get rich from this????**

Tyrell was all:

TYRELL

> **Yaaaa u get paid for views**

Then Amari was like:

TRUTH

U know that baby ate
the meatball?

That baby made BANK

I couldn't believe it! I'd seen that clip of the baby eating the meatball. Whole world had! It was all over the internet.

But I'd never once thought, *Did that baby get RICH eating that meatball?*

I guess he did!

And if that baby got rich . . .

Was I gonna get rich, too?

OH MAN OH MAN!

I wasn't the only one thinking it. Right away, Jazmin texted:

JAZMIN

**U SHARING THAT 💰 💰 💰 WITH US MARCUS???**

Tyrell answered for me:

TYRELL

Heck ya he's gonna share it

TYRELL

**AIN'T THAT RIGHT LITTLE MAN**

What was I gonna say to that? You don't talk back to Tyrell. He made a dope supervillain for a reason. Dude is real-life scary!

So I texted back:

No worries I got you!!!

They all loved that. Went emoji-wild on me:

**JAZMIN**

[emoji reactions]

**KHALID**

[emoji reactions]

**TYRELL**

[emoji reactions]

**AMARI**

**Get that meatball
baby money!!!!** [emoji reactions]

[emoji reactions]

After that, I was so hyped, I had to put my phone down and just run back and forth in my apartment for a while.

My brain was on FIRE. Just thinking that for the first time EVER . . . in my LIFE . . .

I might have ACTUAL MONEY?

It was like getting a jolt of Elektro energy—times ten!

I could buy a new phone! With a battery that didn't die every two minutes!

I could get dope art supplies! And a drawing table!

And comics! I could roll into North Side Comics and buy up all the issues I wanted!

Maybe I'd even make enough for Dad to buy a CAR! Drive us someplace on a vacation!

A place with a swimming pool!

OR...

OH, MAN! What if I could buy us a HOUSE? With its OWN swimming pool?

OH, MAN! OH, MAN!

I checked the numbers on my page.

*817,943*...

How much was MeTube gonna pay me for that? Ten cents a view? A penny?

Could be a lot!

OR...

Maybe it wasn't.

Was Tyrell even right about getting paid for clicks?

How did that work? Did MeTube just send you a check?

I had no idea how it worked!

Or if it even worked at all.

My head got to spinning so hard, I had to lie down on the floor.

I was still lying there when my phone rang.

I figured it was one of the kids from the group text.

But it wasn't. It was Aunt Janice.

She's my dad's sister. And she's always had my back. When *Toothpick Fights the Doom!* only had about twenty views? She was all up in the comments section. Talkin' about "greatest movie ever!" and telling all her friends to watch it.

I don't know if Dad had told her I'd gone viral, or she just saw it herself. But she was over the moon.

"Marcus, I am SO PROUD of you, child! You gettin' it ALL, baby! And you deserve it! Don't listen for a second to that hater in the comments!"

"What hater?" I didn't know about any hater.

"The one in the comment section!" she told me. "But don't you worry! It's just some ignorant fool, got nothing better to do. Don't even read that comment!"

After she said that, I HAD to read the comment. I thanked Aunt Janice. Got off the phone. Started scrolling.

There were about a hundred comments under the movie. All but one of them were hype.

Like, "Love this!"

And "So cute!"

And "Omg dying!"

But the one comment that WASN'T?

It hit me like a slap in the face.

Dude's screen name was "PigFarts_100." This is what he said:

> **@PigFarts_100**
>
> If I ate dog food, and puked it up, and filmed myself puking up the dog food, and put it on MeTube, it would get more clicks than this.

That HURT! 'Cause the dude had put some serious effort into being nasty.

And it wasn't even true! No video of a dude puking up dog food was going to get eight hundred thousand views.

I tried to shoulder shrug it. Pretend I didn't care.

But I couldn't! I don't even know why. There were a hundred comments, all giving me love.

And all I could think about was that ONE nasty one.

It was bringing me down! Stealing my joy! So I jumped in the comments to tell him that:

> **@Marcus_Jenkins**
>
> Why u waste time hating? If u don't like it then don't watch

Three seconds later, he wrote back:

**@PigFarts_100**

I wiped my butt with sandpaper and it was
more fun than watching ur dumb movie

I was like, "COME ON, dude! That is just RUDE."
Then I remembered it was my channel.
I was in control. I could delete his comments!
So I did. Click, click! Made them disappear. Just like that.
A second later, two more comments popped up:

**@PigFarts_100**

U mad bro?

**@PigFarts_100**

U should move to a desert island where u
can be a snowflake cuz everybody hates u

I saw that, and I thought, *Deleting ain't good enough
for this clown!*

So I straight-up BLOCKED him.

Clicked the "Block User from This Channel" button in
the drop menu and BAM!

Goodbye, PigFarts_100! FOREVER.

Five seconds later, another comment popped up:

**@PigFarts_200**

Awwwww widdle baby gawt his feewings hurted

Took me all of three seconds to block PigFarts_200.

Then three more seconds before PigFarts_300 showed up.

**@PigFarts_300**

When u block me, my power grows stronger

**@PigFarts_300**

UR MOVIE STINKS LIKE A DEAD CAT ROTTING ON A PILE OF POOP IN A 100 DEGREE SUN

After that, it just got out of hand.

Before I knew it, it was, like . . . I don't even know. Two hours later?

And I was blocking PigFarts_67000.

That's when Sierra called.

"Maaarcuuus—" She had that schoolteacher-y tone of voice. "What are you doooing?"

"Smacking down a troll in my comments!" I told her.

"Aww, heck, no!" she yelled at me through the phone. "Internet Rule Number One: DO NOT FIGHT TROLLS! All they want is attention! Don't give it to them!"

"I'm not! Just trying to block this fool! But I can't figure out—like, is there a way you can block the name PigFarts plus every number that ever existed?"

"What? Dude, I don't know! That's not even why I'm

calling! I just got back from church, and I got like a hundred messages from Jazmin. Talking 'bout how we all rich now! What did you tell her?"

"That I'd cut her in on the money."

"What money?"

"The money we get from going viral! Like when that baby ate the meatball! I'm finna go past a million views! We gonna get Baby Meatball money!"

I heard her huff out a big old sigh.

"Do you even know how monetization works?" she asked me.

"Course I do!" I yelled.

That was not what you'd call true. Fact was, I'd never even heard that word before.

*Moneti-WHAT?*

"Oh, GOOD," Sierra told me. "Then I don't have to explain to you why those million views are worth ZERO DOLLARS."

## CHAPTER 6

# TURNS OUT I'M NOT ACTUALLY RICH

When Sierra said "ZERO DOLLARS," my whole body went in a slump. Like I was Elektro, and somebody cut my power supply. Let all the juice drain out.

Man, I was right back to being broke again!

"Hold up," I told Sierra. "Can you, like . . . pretend for a minute I DON'T know what you're talking about? Then explain it to me? So I know that you know?"

She gave me another big sigh. Girl was setting a world record for the most sighs in a single day.

"If you want to make money on a MeTube video," she told me, "first you gotta MONETIZE it. That means you tell MeTube to put ADS in front of it. From companies. For products and such. MeTube sells those ads, then they give you a cut of the money.

"But they only do that if your channel is in their Partner Program. So you and MeTube are PARTNERS in making that ad money. And you're not a Partner yet."

"So how do I get to be one?" I asked her.

"You gotta APPLY," she told me. "Or your dad does. 'Cause until you're eighteen, you need a parent or guardian to do it for you."

"OH, MAN!" I said. "I gotta call my dad right now!"

"Slow down!" she said. "No point in doing it yet. 'Cause they won't make you a Partner until you got A THOUSAND SUBSCRIBERS on your channel. When I left for church this morning, you only had about three hundred."

"Bet I got a thousand now!" I told her. "I'm finna get a million views on this video!"

It was true! When I hit refresh, my page views were up over 950,000!

But then I checked my SUBSCRIBER number.

I hadn't looked at that number before. Took me a minute to even find it on the page. It was under my channel name:

## Toothpick_Superhero
410 subscribers

"Dang!" I told her. "I only got four ten."

"That's IT?" Sierra snorted. "You got seven hundred thousand new views since this morning . . . and only a hundred new subscribers? How is that even possible?"

"I don't know! I don't know anything about this stuff!"

Sierra must've been looking at my channel. 'Cause all of a sudden, I heard my own voice coming through the phone:

"*Get yourself over to the* Jazmin Stylez *channel . . . !*"

"Awww, Marcus! What is this nonsense?" Sierra asked.

"I gave Jazmin a shout-out," I said. "Also Amari. And I posted Khalid's stop-motion."

"This is trash, dude!" she told me. "Looks like you're in a hostage video. Like you're tied up in some kidnapper's basement, begging folks for a ransom."

"It's not my fault!" I whined. "I don't know how to do a vlog! I don't even know what that word means."

"Well, it's costing you money," she said.

"How you figure?"

"Here's what I bet happened," said Sierra. "Folks subscribed to you 'cause the *Toothpick* movie's dope. But then you posted three trash videos in a row! And if they've got notifications on, it's like, 'BING! BING! BING! Trash, trash, trash!' Then they're probably thinking, 'I don't need this nonsense in my feed.' So they unsubscribed!"

My body was in a serious slump now. All that Elektro energy was down to zero.

"Are you telling me those vids I put up cost me my Baby Meatball money?" I asked her.

"Yes!" Sierra said. "You gotta delete them."

"I can't delete them! Jazmin will get all mad at me. Khalid and Amari, too!"

"Do you want to make them happy?" Sierra asked. "Or do you want to get rich and famous?"

"Can't I do both?"

"No! You're diluting your brand!"

"What does THAT mean?"

Sierra gave me another world-class sigh. "A BRAND is what you're known for. It's the thing people like about you. And when you post stuff that's not your brand—like these trash hostage videos—it hurts the brand. Makes it weaker. Nobody's going to subscribe to watch ten seconds of Khalid's janky stop-motion movie that's not even done yet."

I sat with that for a second. Tried to get my head around what Sierra was telling me.

"So what you're saying is . . . since my brand is Toothpick . . . I should only post Toothpick movies?"

"If that's what you want your brand to be," said Sierra. "But I don't think your brand should just be Toothpick. 'Cause it takes FOREVER to make a Toothpick movie! That first one took us months! And if you want to get rich and famous on MeTube, you gotta be putting out new content every day."

"Every DAY?"

"AT LEAST twice a week," Sierra told me.

The thought of that made my head hurt. And I didn't even believe it.

"Now, wait just a second," I told her. "Baby Meatball got rich. And he just had that one video. Sitting in his high chair, drooling on that meatball."

"Wrong!" Sierra snorted. "That one video got him his audience. But all the OTHER videos are what made him rich. Check out his channel."

I went back to Dad's laptop. Searched up Baby Meatball on MeTube. Found his channel.

And my mind was BLOWN. That little dude had seven million subscribers!

### Baby_Meatball

7,328,844 subscribers

And he didn't just have the one video. He had THREE HUNDRED of them!

Dude's parents were posting two a week! Just like Sierra said. All kinds of different stuff!

Had titles like, "BABY MEATBALL GETS PRANKED BY HIS BIG SISTER!" And "BABY MEATBALL'S FAVORITE CHEESEBURGER!"

Which kinda seemed like it was made by a cheeseburger company. 'Cause it had a little tag on the video that said, "SPONSORED CONTENT."

Also, Baby Meatball wasn't a baby anymore. Little dude was toddler-size now. Old enough to talk into the camera.

They had him doing video game reviews! Saying stuff in his mush-mouth toddler voice like, *"Awimal Awenue Fwee is my faworite wideo game of AWW TIME! I WUV IT!"*

That one ALSO said "sponsored content." Which made me wonder if Baby Meatball was being straight with us about how good *Animal Avenue 3* was.

He wasn't just making videos, either. He was selling merch! You could buy Baby Meatball T-shirts, Baby Meatball coffee mugs, Baby Meatball meatballs. . . .

Little dude had an EMPIRE!

"Dang!" I told Sierra. "Baby Meatball's been HUSTLING."

"That's how you do it!" Sierra said. "You want to blow up, you gotta put the work in."

I thought about that. And fact: selling Toothpick T-shirts sounded pretty dope.

But the rest of it? I just wasn't feeling that.

"Toothpick's a superhero," I told Sierra. "He saves the world from bad guys. How's he gonna review a cheeseburger?"

"That's why your channel shouldn't just be Toothpick," she told me.

"But that's my brand," I said. "I'm the *Toothpick Superhero* channel!"

"That COULD be your channel," she said. "OR ... you could make it something bigger. A LOT bigger."

"How you figure?"

Sierra got quiet for a minute. Like she was winding up.

"You want to hear my plan?" she asked.

"Course I do!"

"You sure you're ready for it? 'Cause it's BIG. Might be TOO big for you. Fry your little brain."

"Girl, will you just tell me what it is?"

"Okay," she said. "But you better hold on to your butt. 'Cause this is EPIC."

"JUST TELL ME, SIERRA!"

## CHAPTER 7

# SIERRA'S BIG PLAN

"So right now," Sierra said, "you've got your Toothpick channel. And I've got MY channel. Which mostly just has *Phone Zombies* on it."

"That movie was dope!" I said.

And it was! *Phone Zombies* was the movie we made BEFORE *Toothpick Fights the Doom!* It was mostly Sierra's—she wrote it, directed it, and starred in it. But I costarred. It was this horror comedy about a killer smartphone app that turns kids into zombies. When we screened it at the Fall Arts Showcase at our school, kids went nuts for it!

Sierra put it on MeTube, and it got about two thousand page views. That seemed like a lot, until *Toothpick* blew up.

"So here's what I'm thinking," Sierra continued. "We put our two channels together. Go fifty-fifty on it. I'll take down *Phone Zombies* and do a new edit. Split it into chapters. So instead of one movie, it's five episodes. We'll roll those out once a week on our channel. Get the audience hooked on it like a TV show. And while we're doing that, we start making vlogs. Put some of those out every week, too."

"What kind of vlogs?" I asked her.

"I don't know yet," she said. "Could be anything. As long as it's funny. 'Cause that's what our brand should be—it's comedy."

"But my brand is just Toothpick," I said.

She huffed out another sigh. This one had some edge to it.

"Why do you think a million people watched that *Toothpick* movie?" she asked me. "Because it's funny! Like I told you it should be! How many times did we have this fight when we were making it?"

"About a thousand," I said.

It was true. For most of the time we were making the *Toothpick* movie, I'd wanted it to be serious. But Sierra was the director. And she wanted it to be funny. Took me forever to come around and see she was right about that.

"So will you just trust me on this?" she begged. "I'm trying to make us rich here! Don't you want to get rich?"

"Course I do!" I told her. "But I want to do it making Toothpick movies!"

"But they take forever!" she said. "How about you make Toothpick vlogs? Like, I dunno, 'Toothpick's Mailbag,' where you dress up as Toothpick, and you're answering fan mail—"

"Toothpick don't get fan mail!"

"So what? Just make it up! Like a comedy skit. Or, like, you could do 'Toothpick's Superhero Advice Column.' Or 'Toothpick Gets a Toothache—'"

I let out a groan. "That is SO corny! He's a superhero! You want him going to the dentist?"

"You come up with ideas, then!" she told me.

"Like what?" I asked. "'Toothpick Gets Pranked by His Big Sister'? 'Toothpick's Favorite Cheeseburger'?"

"YES!" she yelled.

"NO!" I yelled back. "I hate those ideas!"

I was starting to get hot. 'Cause Toothpick wasn't some joke.

He was SPECIAL. I'd been drawing him for years before I ever met Sierra. When he fought a supervillain, it MATTERED. It was important. Maybe not to anybody else. But to me.

The way Sierra was talking, she just wanted me to turn him into a clown. And yeah, *Toothpick Fights the Doom!* was a funny movie. But it wasn't just clowning. There was more to it than that.

"All I want to do is make another *Toothpick*," I told Sierra. "A sequel. Like the first one."

Sierra lowered her voice, all serious-like. "Marcus, you're not listening: that's gonna take MONTHS. And by the time it comes out, nobody will even remember you! That big audience you just got? It'll be gone! We gotta put new stuff out NOW. Give them a reason to subscribe to the channel!"

"The reason is Toothpick!" I said.

"But you don't HAVE more Toothpick stuff! Dude, this is a once-in-a-lifetime chance. You're going viral! There's a million eyeballs on you! Put out the right content NOW, this week—and you can keep those eyeballs on you. Build your audience. Get rich and famous! We'll do it together! Heck, I'll do most of the work! I'll do all of it! But we gotta do it FAST. And you gotta pivot."

"What's that mean? 'Pivot'?"

"It's a change in direction. You gotta pivot from being just the *Toothpick Superhero* channel to, like, a general comedy channel. So we can put ALL of our stuff out. *Toothpick, Phone Zombies*, the new vlogs we're gonna do . . . We'll call it, like, the *Killer Content Crew*. 'Cause we're a crew! Making content! And it's killer! What do you say?"

I didn't know what to say. It was too much to even think about. My head was swimming.

Plus, my stomach was growling. I needed food. And maybe a nap.

"I gotta eat some lunch," I said. "Let me hit you back later."

"Don't sleep on this," she warned me. "Every second counts! This is our shot!"

"Okay! Okay! Chill."

"Wait!" she said.

"What?"

"Promise me you'll delete those videos? They're killing your brand. No matter what your brand is."

"Ugh! Whatever! I'm out."

After I hung up with Sierra, I went back to my channel. Checked the numbers.

*1,007,023 . . .*

I broke a million! A million people had watched my movie!

But I hardly even got an Elektro zap from it.

Because now all I could think was, *Is Sierra right? Am*

*I messing up my shot to make it big? Are those shout-outs I posted hurting my brand? What even IS a brand?*

I was starting to feel DOWN.

I deleted the three new videos. Clicked the "trash" button next to all of them. Now all I had on my channel was the *Toothpick* movie. I scrolled through the comments on it.

There were a bunch of new ones. Most of them from PigFarts_69000, throwing poop all over me. That got me feeling even more down. I blew out a big sigh. Started deleting them.

Then my phone lit up with texts from Jazmin:

> **MARCUS!!!!**

> **Y U TAKE MY VLOG DOWN???**

> **PUT IT BACK UP!!!!**

My phone started ringing. I didn't even have to look at caller ID to know it was Jazmin.

"Where'd my shout-out go?" she yelled in my ear.

"I had to take it down!" I told her. "It was costing me subscribers!"

"How you figure?"

I didn't want to throw Sierra under the bus. So instead of telling Jazmin the truth, I said, "I got these trolls all up in my comments. I had to take down the vids to get rid of them!"

"Just turn the comments off!" Jazmin told me.

"You can DO that?" I asked her.

"Heck, yeah!" Jazmin showed me how to turn comments off so nobody could post anything under my vids.

Which was good! 'Cause it solved my PigFarts problem once and for all.

But it was also bad. 'Cause then I didn't have an excuse for not putting Jazmin's shout-out vlog back up.

So I UN-deleted the vlog. Put it right back on my channel. I put back Amari's and Khalid's vids, too.

Then I got off the phone and lay down on the couch. Too out of gas to even move. It was late afternoon. I'd been full-time internet famous since breakfast. And I was beat.

Then I heard a knock on the door.

Got up and went to the kitchen, where our front door is. Opened it up.

It was my best friend, J.R.

I started trying to explain what was up. "I just broke a million! And I thought I might be rich! But I ain't. But I could be! If I get a thousand subscribers. Sierra says to do that, I gotta pivot. And I don't know if I want to? Or even what that word means? Or my brand? Which I think is Toothpick. But maybe not? And this dude PigFarts was all up in my comments. First, he was PigFarts One Hundred. Then I blocked him, and he came back as PigFarts Two Hundred! And—why you looking at me like that?"

J.R.'s eyes had been getting smaller and smaller. Like

he was confused. "I thought you just wanted to play some GameBox," he told me.

"Oh!" That seemed like a good idea. Take my mind off all this MeTube business. "Okay. Let's do it."

We sat down on the couch and fired up the GameBox. While *Army of the Undead 3* was loading, I checked my numbers again.

*1,022,349 . . .*

*417 subscribers.*

"So if I got another twenty thousand views," I said to J.R., "and seven more subscribers . . . how many more views do I need to get for, like, six hundred new subscribers? So I can monetize?"

"Wut?" J.R. wrinkled his nose up.

"It's math! Help me do it." For the first time ever, I

was thinking, *Maybe this is why I should be doing my math homework. So I can figure stuff like this out when it comes up.*

"Man, I don't want to do math!" J.R. told me. "I just want to shoot zombies."

So that's what we did.

For about two minutes.

Then my phone started ringing.

I looked at the caller ID. It was Sierra.

Probably calling to yell at me for putting those vids back up.

I turned the ringer off. Put the phone on the couch. A second later, it started buzzing.

I ignored it.

But it kept buzzing.

Over and over.

And over.

And—

"Will you shut that thing off?" J.R. moaned. "Buzzin's driving me nuts!"

I looked at the screen. Sierra had just sent a text:

> CALL ME NOW IT'S IMPORTANT!!!!

"I need a minute," I told J.R.

"We right in the middle, fam! You drop out, these zombies gonna eat my brain!"

"Just gimme a sec," I said. Then I put down the controller and picked up my phone.

Called Sierra.

"I'm busy!" I told her when she picked up.

"Did the dude from *The Helen Show* call you?" she asked.

"The what?"

"*The Helen Show*! Don't you know *The Helen Show*?"

I sure did. EVERYBODY knew *The Helen Show*. Biggest talk show ever! Weekday afternoons. Back when my mama was still alive, it was her favorite thing on TV!

"Course I know *The Helen Show*!" I told Sierra. "What about it?"

"The producer called! They want US to be guests on it!"

# CHAPTER 8

# THE HELEN SHOW

"AAAAAAAAH!" I yelled so loud, J.R. smacked me in the arm.

"Fam! You busted my eardrums!" J.R. had his face bunched up like a crab.

"They want us to be on *The Helen Show*!" I yelled.

"Well, good for you," he said. "But I got zombies on my butt! Help me get them off!"

I left J.R. to the game. Took my phone and charger to the bedroom so I could talk to Sierra in private.

"Just what is going on here?" I asked her.

"Dude from *The Helen Show* DM'd me. Said he wants us on the show. So I called—"

"Why'd he DM YOU?" I wanted to know.

"'Cause you didn't answer him!"

"He didn't DM me!"

"You sure about that? Check your ClickChat."

"Hang on." I couldn't check ClickChat on my phone and talk at the same time. So I ran back to the living room to get Dad's laptop.

J.R. was still on the couch, holding the GameBox controller and looking salty.

"I just died, fam! Are we playing or not?"

"Play without me," I told him.

"That ain't no fun!" he said. But I was already headed back to the bedroom.

I opened up the laptop. Checked my ClickChat DMs. There it was, from a few hours back:

**@Helen_Show**

Hi, Marcus! I'm a producer on The Helen Show. We LOVE your movie and would like to talk about having you on the show to tell Helen all about how you made it. If you're interested, can you please have your parent

or guardian get in touch with me ASAP so
we can work out the details?
Sincerely, Chad Darlington

"MAN OH MAN!" I yelled. Dude had left a phone number and everything!

"You gotta have your dad call him," Sierra told me. "Soon as you can! My mama talked to him already. He's sending over a contract."

"What we need a contract for?"

"He told my mom it's so we go on *Helen* first. And not other shows."

"What other shows?"

"I dunno. *Mandy*? *Terry and Tessa*?"

"They gonna have us on, too?"

"I dunno. But for *Helen*, they need your dad to sign the contract. They're saying they'll put us on this week."

"THIS WEEK?"

"Yeah! They want us to come in and tape the show on Tuesday morning! Put it on the air Wednesday afternoon."

"OH MAN OH MAN!"

I jumped off with Sierra to call Dad. He didn't answer. So I started texting him:

DAD DAD DAD

CALL ME NOW!!!

I went on like that for about twenty more texts. Just couldn't help it.

ZAAAP! I had that Elektro energy going again! It was frying my circuits!

Dad didn't answer. Drove me nuts!

I went back out to the living room so I could pace around some more.

J.R. was gone. Guess he didn't want to play GameBox without me.

I was on my seven-zillionth trip around the apartment when Dad finally called. He sounded scared.

"Marcus! What's wrong?"

"*THE HELEN SHOW!*" I told him. "They want us to come on TV! You gotta call the producer dude!"

For a couple seconds, Dad didn't say anything. When he did, he was low-key. But it was an angry kind of low-key.

"Son, that is NOT an emergency. Emergency is, 'I broke my leg.' Or 'The house is on fire.'"

"This is important, Dad!"

"So's my job, son! Can't be talking on the phone in the middle of a shift!"

"I'm sorry! But Sierra's mom already talked to them! They gotta send us a contract—"

"They can wait," he told me. "Till my shift is over. This probably ain't even real."

"It's real, Dad! You gotta call 'em!"

"When my shift is done."

"But, Dad!"

"Enough! You gonna make me lose my job, boy!"

When I heard that, I finally settled down.

"I'm sorry, Dad."

"It's okay. I got you soon as my shift ends."

It took FOREVER for that shift to end. Even though it was probably just an hour or so. I spent the time checking my numbers. Running up and down the hallway. And lying on the couch, just being amazed.

Was I really going to be on *The Helen Show*?

I thought back to when Mama was alive. On days when she had an evening shift at the hospital, she'd watch *Helen* before she went to work. When I was little, I used to rest my head on her lap and watch it with her.

Remember that one time Helen bought a whole car for everybody in her studio audience? And they all flipped out? Started crying?

Made my mama cry, too. I remember her sitting on the couch, shaking her head and wiping her tears.

"That Helen is something special," Mama said. "Just look at all that joy she's spreading."

And now I was going to be on that show, maybe?

MAN!

As I kept thinking about it, my stomach started to get flippy. Like I was scared.

Or maybe just hungry. So much had been happening, I never got around to eating anything except that one bowl of cereal in the morning.

Finally, Dad texted me:

What's your burger order

CALL THE HELEN SHOW!!!!

That's not a menu item

Hurry up I'm next in line

Double cheeseburger fries. CALL THEM!!!!!

I texted Dad the *Helen* dude's phone number. All Dad texted back was a thumbs-up.

I was losing it!

I was starving to death, too. Getting all shaky.

Finally, Dad came home with the burgers and some news.

"So I talked to the dude. Seems like he maybe is actually real."

"COURSE HE'S REAL, DAD!"

"Settle! Let me explain. They want you and Sierra to come to their studio, tape the show on Tuesday morning. Can you miss school for that?"

"OF COURSE I CAN! OH MY GOSH!"

"All right, then. Producer said he'd email me the contract. Soon as we eat dinner, I'll take a look at it. Get everything squared away. All right?"

"Can't you square it away now?"

"Son, I been working all day. It can wait twenty minutes. Now, let's sit down and eat."

It seemed fair. I mean, I WAS starving.

"Okay! Okay. Thank you, Dad!"

"It's all good. Why don't you plate that food while I get changed?"

Dad went to the bedroom to switch out of his work clothes. I got dinner plates out. Put the burgers and fries on them. Poured us both glasses of water from the tap.

I was sitting down at the table when Dad came back. Gave me a look.

"What?" I asked him. "What'd I do?"
"Where's the laundry, son?"
OH, MAN!
I forgot the laundry!

## CHAPTER 9

# IT'S HARD TO DO LAUNDRY WHEN YOU'RE BLOWING UP

It's hard to do other stuff, too. Like eating. And sleeping. And homework.

But especially laundry. Soon as Dad reminded me, I ran to the basement. J.R.'s mom must've done hers on Saturday instead, because that first load I put in was still in the machine. After sitting in there locked up all day, it had this weird stink on it. Like it didn't smell clean anymore.

So I had to rerun the whole load. Then I went back upstairs and finally got that burger in my mouth. It was cold by then. But I was so hungry, I didn't care.

Three bites in, Sierra started texting me.

> Why'd u repost those videos????

> And r u going to let me share ur channel?

> We need to move FAST so it's ready when Helen airs

I didn't even text back. Just rolled my eyes and made a *huugh!* sound.

"What's the matter?" Dad asked me.

"Sierra's trying to boss me. Says I gotta change my channel name so we can put all of her stuff on it, too."

"What's your channel name?"

"*Toothpick Superhero.* And that's all I want it to be! I don't want to make some dumb vlogs like, 'Watch Me Prank My Neighbor!' Or 'Lemme Talk About This Pimple on My Nose for Ten Minutes.'"

"So don't," Dad said.

"But Sierra says if all I do is Toothpick, I ain't gonna make money."

Dad wrinkled up his nose. "Who said anything about making money?"

"You can make bank, Dad!" I told him. "Folks on MeTube get rich! But you gotta, like, post videos every day or something."

"Why don't you just post more Toothpick movies?"

"They're too hard to make," I told him. "You want them to be good, it takes time."

Dad chewed some French fries and thought it over for a bit.

"Seems to me," he said, "you should just keep doing what you're doing. If Toothpick's good enough to get you on *The Helen Show*? I mean, shoot! Why mess with success?"

Hearing Dad say that made me feel a lot better. The burger and fries were helping, too. I stuffed my face for a while. Then I got to wondering something:

"Hey, Dad . . . what do you think Mama would say if she knew I was going on *Helen*?"

Dad gave a little chuckle. Then he leaned back in his chair, looking sad and happy at the same time.

"Oh, man . . ." he said. "She'd just be over the moon. SO proud of you! She loved that show!"

"I know, right?" I got a little lump in my throat. Had to wash it down with some water. "Just wish she could be here. To see me on it."

"I'll tell you what," Dad said. "I bet she WILL see it."

"You think so?" I asked him. "Think they got TV in heaven?"

Dad laughed. "You kidding? It's heaven, son! They got everything! Cable TV. High-speed internet. Don't you worry. Your mama's going to see every second of that show."

After dinner, I switched the laundry while Dad looked over the contract. Worked things out on the phone with the producer dude. Said they'd send a car first thing Tuesday morning to pick us up and take us to the show. Dad checked with his boss, got himself the day off work to come along.

It was really going to happen! Sierra and I were going to be on *The Helen Show*!

Once I knew it was real, I got excited.

But then I got SCARED.

It was like . . . you ever climb up a really tall ladder? And you're feeling on top of the world—but then you look down? And you realize how far you could fall?

That's how I felt, thinking about going on *The Helen Show*. What if I messed up? Got tongue-tied? Said the wrong thing? In front of the whole world?

No joke: I got so scared, I couldn't sleep that night.

Couldn't stop getting up to check my page views, either. They'd leveled off around a million point two. And five hundred subscribers.

Looking at that subscriber number, I got to worrying again about everything Sierra had said.

How was I going to get those followers up past a thousand so I could monetize? If I didn't put out a dope new Toothpick movie, I could lose that whole audience! Blow my shot!

I went back to bed. Couldn't even close my eyes. I was freaking out! Excited, scared, and worried all at once.

Then I asked myself: *What would Toothpick do if I was him?*

*If I was a superhero, how would I handle this?*

That's when the idea came to me.

A brand-new Toothpick story! With a brand-new villain! The perfect movie sequel!

I jumped out of bed. Got my drawing stuff out. Started going to town.

I had a story in me! And there was no getting to sleep until I put it all down on paper.

## CHAPTER 10

# THE BATTLE ON THE BUS

"This is the worst idea I ever heard," Sierra told me.

"IT'S GENIUS!" I yelled so loud the whole packed-in city bus turned their heads and gave me dirty looks.

Little old lady right in front of us gave me a "SSSHHH!"

Sierra was shaking her head and rolling her eyes. "Dude. A supervillain named *Stink Pig*?"

"Yes! Check these pages out!" I pulled the new comic I'd drawn out of my backpack and showed it to her. "See, everybody loves Toothpick. 'Cause he saved them from the Doom! But then this Stink Pig dude comes to town, tries to turn folks against him. Spreads stink gas all over the city. Like rotten eggs and chili farts. Blames it all on Toothpick!

"But Toothpick beats him down! Makes the smell go away! Everybody loves him even more! And the BEST part is—Amari's already got a pig mask. From that video he shot last month. So we got the costume all ready to go! We can start shooting today!"

Sierra gave me a look like, *No way.* "You going to shoot a whole movie in one afternoon?"

"Not the whole movie," I told her. "Just a teaser! Like a two-minute sneak preview! *Toothpick Fights the Stink Pig!* We can shoot part of a fight scene with me and Amari going at it. Put it up right away. Get folks hyped for the full movie. Then we'll shoot the rest of it this weekend!"

My head was spinning, I was so excited!

Some of that head spinning might have just been lack of sleep. I hadn't gotten more than a couple hours. So I was feeling squeezed-out and sour-stomached.

But I was raring to go! Nothing could stop me!

Except Sierra's bad attitude.

"First of all," she told me in that know-it-all, school-teacher voice of hers. "Nobody cares about that troll in your comments except you."

"This ain't about me!" I told her. "It's about Toothpick!"

"Well, you should tell Toothpick to quit reading his comment section."

"It ain't about the comment section! It's a superhero story! And it's fresh! You ever seen a villain mess people up with stink gas before?"

"There's a reason for that," Sierra told me.

"'Cause nobody ever thought of it!" I said.

"OR . . ." Girl was rolling her eyes at me. "Maybe 'cause it's no fun to watch."

"What you mean, 'no fun'?"

"Think about it, Marcus: movies are what you SEE and HEAR. If you can't see it or hear it, how you gonna put it in a movie? What's it gonna be? Bunch of folks walking around with their noses wrinkled, going 'Eeeeeew, beef'?"

Little old lady in front of us turned around again. "She makes a good point, son. Nobody wants to see that."

I felt like telling that little old lady to mind her own business. But I didn't. 'Cause I have respect for little old ladies.

"You want to hear MY idea for new content?" Sierra asked me.

"I don't know," I said. "Do I?"

"Here it is: BTS."

"What's that mean? BTS?"

"Short for 'behind the scenes.' We'll make a whole series out of going on *The Helen Show*. Film ourselves driving to the studio. Going backstage. All of it."

"I don't know," I said. "What's good about that?"

"We'll make it good," she said. "Plus, I got an idea for a vlog. It's called *Tall Girl Troubles*. I'll talk about all the stuff that's hard about being the tallest girl in class."

"That idea's terrible!" I told her.

Fact: I didn't know if *Tall Girl Troubles* was a bad idea or not. I just knew I didn't want it on my channel. And I was mad as heck at Sierra for trashing my Stink Pig idea.

"You don't know nothing!" she shot back at me. "And you don't have to like it. Just let me put out my stuff, and you can put out your stuff."

"Put out what you want," I told her. "Just keep it off my channel."

"Don't you want to make it OUR channel?" she asked me. "The *Killer Content Crew?*"

"I'm not feeling that," I said. "I just want my channel to be Toothpick."

Sierra didn't like the sound of that at all. Her mouth got all twisted up like she was fixing to go off. I watched her take a deep breath. Trying to calm herself down. "So you don't want to get rich and famous?" she hissed at me.

"Yeah, I do," I said. "But with Toothpick! That's what got us this far. Why mess with success?"

She snorted. "Do you even know why you're successful? 'Cause of ME, Marcus. 'Cause I directed your movie!"

She wasn't wrong. But I just didn't want all that other stuff on my channel. "If you want to do *Tall Girl Behind the Scenes*," I told her, "why don't you put it on your own channel?"

"My channel's got two thousand views!" she yelled. "You got a MILLION!"

Folks on the bus were turning around to look at us again. Sierra was getting hot. And so was I. 'Cause all of a sudden, it felt like she was trying to get over on me.

"So that's how it is?" I asked her. "You just trying to steal my page views?"

"They're mine, too!" she shot back. "Your movie's only good 'cause I MADE IT GOOD."

That set me off. 'Cause the thing about me is, if somebody pushes my buttons too hard? I get like Wolf Boy.

You know that superhero? Whenever he gets too mad, he turns into a werewolf? Grows some fangs? Gets all hairy? Starts tearing up everything in sight?

I'm the same way, just on the inside. And when Sierra said she was the only reason my *Toothpick* movie was good?

I got Wolf Boy mad at that!

"I was drawing Toothpicks before I ever met you!" I snarled.

"And that's ALL you were doing!" she snarled back. "If it weren't for me, all you'd have is a notebook full of dumb comics."

*DUMB?* Oh, man! Girl made me so mad, I couldn't even make words. I just spit out some Wolf Boy growls. "GRARRH! HRRGH! Heck with you!"

"Heck with YOU," Sierra said. "That movie's half mine at least! I should sue you for it!"

"I'll sue YOU!" I told her.

Little old lady turned around again. "Sounds like you kids gonna end up in court," she said. "Ought to get yourselves on *The Judge Jenny Show.*"

I took a deep breath. Calmed myself down. Got Wolf Boy back in his cage.

"We can't go on *Judge Jenny,*" I said. "'Cause we just signed a contract with *The Helen Show.* They want us exclusive."

Little old lady thought I was lying. I would've set her straight, but then Sierra kicked me in the foot to shut me up.

## CHAPTER 11

# HERO OF THE HALLWAYS

Sierra and I didn't speak a word the whole rest of that bus ride. Just sat and sulked with our arms crossed. I was still burning up at her when we got off at the stop near school.

I couldn't believe she called my comics dumb!

But I'll tell you what: part of what got me all twisted up was thinking she was right.

Until Sierra came along, I didn't know the first thing about making a movie.

I STILL barely knew how to make one! She was the brains in that department.

And I could see how she was right about Stink Pig. How was I gonna make a movie about a smell? That was just janky.

Maybe she was right about the channel, too. Maybe I should share it with her after all.

Except I didn't want to do all that other stuff! Those ideas just seemed corny. Why couldn't she put them on her own channel?

Wasn't my fault *Toothpick* went viral instead of one of her movies.

I mean, if *Phone Zombies* had gone viral instead, I wouldn't be all up in Sierra's face, trying to get her to put my stuff on her channel!

Actually, that wasn't true. I probably WOULD be begging her for a repost.

Oh, man . . .

The whole situation was making my brain hurt.

Plus, I was dead tired. That lack of sleep was catching up to me. By the time I walked into school, I could barely keep my eyes open.

But then I started down the hall to my locker. And I noticed something.

Something strange.

Kids were looking at me different. Even kids I didn't know were turning their heads my way.

Whispering to each other. Smiling at me.

Word must've spread about *Toothpick* going viral. And it changed things. I could feel this low-key buzz in the air.

It was like that Elektro energy I got from all the page views!

Except this was even better. 'Cause it wasn't just numbers on a screen. It was real people giving me love! Sending me good vibes! Showing respect!

I'd never felt anything like that! It was amazing!

I was putting my coat in my locker. And this girl, Maya, came up to me. I only knew her a little. And she was all, "Yo, is it true you know Tevin Bart?"

And I was like, "Sorta . . . I mean, he's a fan."

Which was true! He'd said as much in his ClickChat post!

Then Maya was all, "Can you tell him to follow me on ClickChat? So I can DM him?"

I didn't know what to say to that. Tevin Bart didn't even follow ME on ClickChat. But I didn't want to look a fool in front of Maya.

So I just said, "I'll see what I can do."

She gave me a big old smile for that.

Then I went to math class. Just before it started, this kid Derek was like, "Fam! I heard you gonna be in the next Tevin Bart movie!"

Whole class looked at me like, "WUUUUT?"

I could tell they were hyped! And what was I going to do? Let them down?

So I just gave Derek a shrug and said, "It's possible."

'Cause it was! I mean, anything is possible. Right?

So technically, I wasn't even lying.

Then class started. I couldn't really pay attention. My brain was too busy puzzling out what to do about Sierra and my channel.

By now, I wasn't tired anymore. I was amped! Riding high on that Elektro attention energy I got from the other kids!

And I wanted to keep it going! Crank out a trailer for the sequel! Keep those eyes on me!

Couldn't be Stink Pig. Sierra was right. That was just corny.

Except . . . it HAD to be Stink Pig. Or something like him.

'Cause I couldn't get that PigFarts punk out of my head. I was SO burned up at him! Spreading his nasty business all over my comments.

If that nasty stuff couldn't be a smell? On account of you can't show smell in a movie? Then what could it be?

Maybe barf?

No. Yuck! That was just gross.

What if it was a sound?

That seemed better. Closer to the truth, too. Like a dude who spits insults all day. Got an annoying voice. Like an alarm clock. Or a busted machine. Sounds like gears grinding.

Like a robot.

Yeah! A busted-up robot!

Spitting insults so loud, he breaks people's eardrums!

*"KRANK-KRANK-KRANK . . . YOU STINK LIKE A DEAD CAT! KRANK-KRANK-KRANK . . ."*

That sounded like a dope villain!

So what did this robot look like?

Was he a giant? Ten feet tall?

Nah. Too hard to film that.

A regular-size robot. Yeah!

We could make a costume from a garbage can! Maybe some tinfoil!

What should I call him?

The Hatebot!

No, even better:

THE HATEBOT 3000!

I started drawing him in my math notebook.

Spent the whole rest of the school day drawing Hatebot 3000s in my notebooks. Coming up with ideas for the teaser.

Also napping. I was bone-tired. I conked out for a while near the end of math.

Then again partway through science.

Plus most of social studies.

I couldn't help it. I needed those naps. Had to get refreshed!

As soon as school let out, I had a teaser to make!

# CHAPTER 12

# FILM CLASS FIGHT CLUB

When school ended, I hustled over to the room where these two college kids, Darren and Trish, teach the Afternoon Adventures filmmaking class. I was in their class until I got kicked out a while back. That's a long story. No point in getting into it.

I was a little worried they wouldn't let me in the door. But they'd heard about the *Toothpick* movie going viral, and they were hyped to see me.

"There he is!" Darren yelled. "The King of the World! Congratulations, brother!"

"MY HERO!" screamed Trish. "You broke the internet!"

"It's been pretty wild," I told them.

Darren nodded. "I bet it has! You just dropping by to say hello? Let us know you didn't forget the little people now you're all famous?"

"I'm looking for the other kids," I told them. "Trying to get them together to make a teaser for the *Toothpick* sequel."

Just then, Jazmin walked in and started tearing into me:

"Marcus! Why didn't you tell *The Helen Show* to have ME on, too?"

It was a good question. Truth was, I hadn't even thought of it. "I didn't think I could do that," I told her.

"What's this about *The Helen Show*?" Trish asked.

"He's gonna be on it!" Jazmin explained. "Sierra, too! But they forgot to invite ME!"

Darren and Trish looked at me like I'd just won the lottery.

"Good on you, Marcus!" Darren beamed.

"That's amazing!" Trish shrieked.

"He's gonna LOOK amazing," said Jazmin. "'Cause I'm doing his hair and makeup! Gonna film it as a collab for the *Jazmin Stylez* channel!"

"You're going to what now?" It was the first I'd heard of this makeup business.

"You gotta let me style you, Marcus!" Jazmin told me. "Sierra said yes to it already! And you owe me a collab!"

"But I don't need my hair done," I said. "I barely have hair."

"Then I'll do your makeup."

"I don't need makeup!"

"Heck you don't! Boy, you're all kinds of ashy."

Trish was still shaking her head like she was amazed. "I can't believe this! You're going to be on TV!"

I was thinking, *On TV wearing MAKEUP? Nobody told me I had to do THAT.*

But before I could say anything, Amari showed up and got on me just like Jazmin had:

"Yo, Marcus! You gotta get Helen to play my new track!"

"What?"

"C'mon, man! It's a banger!"

"I don't think I can tell Helen what kind of music to play," I said.

"Don't be like that! C'mon! I'll let you guest rap on my next one. We'll collab!"

I was about to tell Amari I don't even know how to rap. But then Khalid came in the room just in time to hear Amari say "collab." So he chimed in:

"Will you collab with me, too? We could make a Toothpick stop-motion!"

Man, I couldn't believe it. Before yesterday, none of these kids ever said a word about a collab. Now they were all over me!

"Can we just shoot a Toothpick teaser first?" I asked them. "And THEN do collabs? I got a dope idea! *Toothpick Fights the Hatebot 3000!*"

They all rolled their eyes at me.

"We already DID a Toothpick!" said Amari.

"But don't you want me to get past a thousand subscribers?" I asked them. "So we can monetize? I'll share the money with you!"

Sierra walked in while I was saying that. "You gonna share your channel, too?" she wanted to know.

Jazmin's eyebrows jumped halfway up her forehead. "Ohmygosh! YES! Share your channel with us! We'll ALL share it!"

I groaned. *Not this again!*

"But it's the *TOOTHPICK* channel!" I told them.

"That ain't fair," said Amari. "We ALL worked on that movie."

"We all worked on EVERYTHING," I told him. "I helped you out with all your music videos! I did Jazmin's titles for her! Filmed her how-tos! Helped Khalid with his stop-motion! And if any of YOU went viral? I wouldn't go trying to make you share your channels with ME. Why can't we just do collabs? Keep on helping each other?"

"If you wanted to help us, why'd you try to take down our shout-outs?" Jazmin asked me.

I pointed at Sierra. "She told me to!"

"What now?" Everybody gave Sierra the stink eye.

Sierra gave it right back to me. "Don't listen to him!" she told the others. "He's just trying to distract you. From the fact that he won't share his channel."

"I'll share the money from it," I said. "I promise! If y'all help me make a new Toothpick teaser, I can get to a thousand followers. Then we can monetize!"

"Why don't you just monetize our collabs?" Jazmin asked me.

"'Cause nobody wants to see those!" I told her.

I didn't mean that the way it sounded. But they ALL got hot. Thought I was dissing them.

"Boy, you think you're all that, don't you?" Jazmin snapped.

"Dude goes viral, thinks he's king of the world!" snarled Amari.

"It ain't like that!" I said. "It's just, y'know, like . . . my brand is Toothpick—"

They all rolled their eyes. "Listen to this fool!" Amari yelled. *"My brand!"*

"That's just what SHE said!" I pointed to Sierra again.

Sierra tried to look all innocent. "Don't put this on me."

"It IS you!" I said. "I didn't even know what a brand was until you told me!"

"I wish somebody was filming this fight," said Trish. "'Cause it'd make a dope reality show."

When Sierra heard that, her eyes got wide. "That's a great idea!" She pulled her phone out and held it up. "Can we do it again? And film it this time?"

"NO!" I yelled.

Just then, the after-school bell rang. That's the bell that says: if you're in Afternoon Adventures, you should be in class. And if you're NOT in Afternoon Adventures, you need to get your butt out of school.

"I hate to break up the reality show," said Darren. "But technically, Marcus is not supposed to be here after the bell rings."

I gave it one more shot. "Doesn't anybody want to make a Toothpick teaser?" I begged them.

They didn't even answer. Just folded their arms and shook their heads.

I didn't know what to say to that. So I turned around and left.

My head was spinning when I walked out of school.

I didn't know if I was being a fool . . . or if they were.

And why'd Sierra hang me out to dry like that? Why didn't she have my back?

She was the one who said we needed to get new content out fast. So why wouldn't she help me make a Toothpick teaser? It'd be a hundred times better than posting some dumb film class fight!

Why wouldn't any of them help? Why were they so mad at me? Were they just jealous?

Or was it on me? Was I being selfish? Should I be sharing my channel with them?

But it was MY channel!

All I could think was, *If I can shoot that Toothpick teaser myself . . . put it online, get past a thousand subscribers . . . monetize, get that money . . . I can share it with the other kids. And they'll see what fools they're being!*

Trouble was, I couldn't shoot a teaser by myself.

Who could I get to help me? Who could play the Hatebot 3000?

I was so lost in my head, walking up that sidewalk to the bus stop, I didn't see Tyrell until he was on top of me.

All six feet two, two hundred and fifty pounds of him. Looking SCARY.

"Where's my money, Little Man?" he growled.

## CHAPTER 13

# TYRELL GIVES ME THE STRONG ARM

Tyrell was taking up the whole sidewalk, right between me and where I needed to go to catch the bus home. Sly, Naz, and Double D were backing him up like usual.

I felt like a mouse. Staring up at a cat. That was fixin' to eat me.

My voice even squeaked like a mouse. "What up, Tyrell?"

"My bank account is what's up," he said. "Soon as you pay me for my services."

I got weak in the knees. Started babbling. "I got you, dude! Except—y'know—thing is—turns out—I mean, MeTube, man!—those dudes won't let you monetize unless you got a thousand subscribers. And I only got five hundred!"

"That's a you problem," said Tyrell. "Not a me problem. So YOU need to pay ME right now. Unless you want TWO problems."

My whole body was turning to jelly. "I got you, T! For certain! But I can't get money till MeTube pays me!"

"Get it from Flitter, then," Tyrell told me.

*What?*

"I ain't even on that site," I said.

"Heck you ain't. Half my feed's Toothpick memes! Show him a flit, Naz."

Naz pulled his phone out. Thumb punched it a couple times. Then he held out the screen to show me his Flitter app.

Some dude had posted a flit with a GIF in it—y'know, one of those short little video memes? Couple seconds long, running on a loop with no sound?

The one Naz showed me was from *Toothpick Fights the Doom!* I was in my costume, jumping off a playground slide and karate-kicking Tyrell as the Doom. Knocking him on his butt.

I had no clue how that meme even got made. But it was amazing! I was a Flitter star, and I didn't even know it! I got so excited, I forgot for a sec that Tyrell was fixin' to stomp me.

"That's dope!" I told him. "Ain't it?"

"Oh, for sure," said Tyrell. "That's why you gotta pay me for it. I need to be compensated. For the use of my image."

"I don't think it works that way," I said.

"It does now," Tyrell told me. "Because I said so."

"But, like, Flitter ain't just gonna send me money—"

"See, that's another YOU problem," said Tyrell.

"Sure is," said Sly.

"True dat," Naz agreed.

"Call it an MP!" Double D suggested.

Everybody looked at him.

"What's that mean?" Tyrell asked.

"MP!" Double D repeated. "Short for 'Marcus Problem!'"

Tyrell gave him a big old grin. "Oh, that's good! Made it short like he is. I like that." Then he turned back to me. "Y'all can solve your MP however you want," he said. "Long as you get me my money."

"You'll get it!" I told him. "Soon as I hit a thousand followers!"

"No, see, that's another MP. What you gotta do is give me my money NOW."

"I ain't got money, Tyrell! And I ain't gonna unless I can get home and shoot a teaser so I can—WHATCHUDOIN', MAN?"

Halfway through my sentence, Tyrell grabbed me by the waist, picked me up, spun me upside down, tossed me in the air, and caught my ankles on the way down.

So in half a second, I went from looking UP at his face to looking DOWN at his legs. And when I looked up, over my head? Instead of seeing sky, I saw sidewalk. I could feel all the blood rushing to my head, making my face swell up.

Tyrell shook me out until my pockets emptied. Sly and Naz picked up everything that came out.

"What we got?" Tyrell asked them.

"Let's see," said Sly. "Got a student ID . . . bus pass . . . hundred-year-old phone . . . and some house keys."

"Bus pass got money on it?"

"Nope. One of them student ones."

"How about the phone?" Tyrell asked. "That worth something?"

I watched from upside down as Naz pressed some buttons on my phone. "Naw, man. It's bricked."

Tyrell huffed out a big sigh. Then he turned me right-side up and set my feet back on the sidewalk.

"That is just sad, Little Man. We gonna have to put you on the installment plan. Bring some cash tomorrow, or you gonna wish you did."

Naz and Sly gave me my stuff back. Then the four of them started to walk off.

"Wait!" I said.

Tyrell stopped and turned around. "What?"

I'd just had an idea. Didn't know if it was a bad idea or a good idea. But I said it anyway:

"Y'all want to help me make a Toothpick video?"

## CHAPTER 14

# THE TERRIFYING TEASER

At first, getting Tyrell and his crew to help me shoot the teaser seemed like the best idea I'd ever had. They were into it! Tyrell couldn't play the Hatebot 3000. 'Cause in the Toothpick movie universe, he was already the Doom. So Sly, Naz, and Double D spent the whole bus ride back to my neighborhood arguing over who'd be the best robot.

"I got the voice for it!" Naz said. "CLANKETY-CLANK-CLANK!"

"But check this!" Double D told him. "I can robot dance!"

He could, too! He showed us some moves in the bus aisle.

Then Sly washed them both.

"I got the whole package, yo! GZANK-A-DANK-CLANK-A-DANK-DANK!"

He put a robot voice together with some robot moves. And man, it was gold!

"We got a winner!" Tyrell announced. I had to agree.

We got off the bus near my place. I ran ahead and changed into my Toothpick costume at home. It's mostly just sweats that are too small, plus a long-sleeve shirt with the Toothpick logo on the chest. But it looks pretty dope.

I plugged my phone in to recharge it. Then I met Tyrell and his crew back downstairs on my stoop to talk over the shoot.

That's when the trouble started.

"What about MY costume?" Sly asked me. "How you gonna make me look like a robot?"

"I got you, man!" I told him. My building's got a couple of big metal garbage cans under the front stairs that we put out on trash day. I went behind the stairs and picked the cleanest-looking one.

It was not what you'd call "extremely clean." It was more like "half clean." Or maybe "a third clean."

Plus, there were a couple bags of garbage in it already. I took those out, picked up the empty can, and brought it out to show Sly.

"All we gotta do is turn this upside down and put it on your head—"

"Awww, heck, no!" said Sly.

Except he didn't say "heck." He said a word I can't repeat.

The other dudes started laughing.

"Garbage head!"

"Trash boy!"

"Better put a can liner on that dome, son!"

Just like that, I lost my costar. I tried to argue it, but Sly wasn't going to budge.

Naz and Double D didn't want to put a garbage can on their head to play the Hatebot 3000, either.

"Man, somebody's gotta do it!" I told them.

Then Tyrell had a very bad idea.

"Just fight the can," he said.

"What you mean?" I asked him.

"You stand there, being Toothpick," he said. "And we'll stay off camera. Make robot noises. Then we'll throw the can at you. Be like you getting attacked by a flying robot."

"Yaaas!" said Naz.

"Dope!" said Sly.

"Let's do it!" said Double D.

"Let's NOT do it!" I said.

But they did it. Pushed me into the street. Set themselves up on either sidewalk. And started chucking the garbage can at me.

It was bad news. I was jumping and ducking. Screaming for them to stop. And thinking, *Man, it can't get worse than this*.

Then one of them got the idea to bring out the second can from behind the stairs.

And it turned out it COULD get worse. 'Cause then it was TWO barrels getting thrown at me.

They'd yell "CLANKETY-CLANK!" while they tossed them at my head.

I'd yell back, "STOP!"

And "HELP!"

And "THIS AIN'T COOL, MAN!"

Then they'd yell stuff like, "Be Toothpick!" And "Fight them trash cans! You a superhero!"

Sly kept yelling, "Be Donkey Kong!" I didn't even know what that meant.

I guess the whole thing was funny to them. 'Cause they could not stop laughing.

It wasn't funny to me. It was scary.

And tiring. I got a workout dodging those cans!

Tyrell filmed the whole thing on his phone. Once they finally had enough, the four of them sat down on my stoop to watch the clips. Had themselves a whole OTHER round of laughing at me.

"Don't look so sad, Little Man!" Tyrell told me. "We got some comedy GOLD here."

"Can you send me the clips for my teaser?" I asked him.

"I could. If you pay me for them."

"I ain't got no money, Tyrell!"

"Then you ain't got no clips, son. This here's my intellectual property."

After a while, Tyrell and his boys got bored and went off to give somebody else a hard time.

I was so tired from ducking those barrels, I couldn't even find the energy to stand up and go inside. Just sat there on the stoop feeling sorry for myself while my eye-lids got heavy.

It was about half an hour till sunset. There was no way I was gonna get a teaser shot that day.

Until J.R. came home from basketball practice.

"Why you sitting out here, fam?"

I started to tell him all the reasons my day had gone in the toilet.

But then I realized: J.R. could save me!

"Hey, man—how'd you like to be an INTERNET STAR?"

J.R. looked doubtful. "I dunno. You an internet star—and you looking pretty ragged right now."

"Please!" I begged him. "I just need fifteen minutes, dude! You'd be saving my life!"

I could tell J.R. wasn't into it.

But he's also my best friend.

And that counts for something.

He gave me a shoulder shrug. "Aaaite. What you need me to do?"

## CHAPTER 15

# TEASER TAKE TWO!

"You sure this is gonna work, fam?"

We were at the playground a few blocks from home. I was trying to get my phone balanced just right on a park bench so it could shoot me and J.R. fighting.

But I had to angle it so I'd shoot just the TOP half of J.R. 'Cause we didn't have a costume for his bottom half. So it was just his legs in basketball shorts, sticking out the bottom of the can.

And that did not look robot-like. Ain't no Hatebot 3000 wears basketball shorts. So I had to make sure everything on J.R. that was below the can stayed out of the frame.

Had to get the shot right on the first try, too. 'Cause I figured my phone would only shoot for a couple minutes before the battery quit on me.

Plus, it was getting dark. So the sun was ALSO only good for a couple more minutes.

I got the phone lined up just right. Then I showed J.R.

where to stand off camera. Put a fast-food wrapper down about ten feet away, right where I wanted him to fight me.

"It's gonna be great!" I told him. "You start over there. When I yell 'action,' you do some robot yelling. Then—"

"What you mean, 'robot yelling'?" he asked.

"I dunno! Like, 'CLANKY-CLANK!' Except your whole supervillain thing is, you spit insults. So make it nasty. Like, 'FILTHY FILTHIN' CLANKY-CLANK!'"

J.R.'s eyes got all narrow, like he was confused. "'Filthy filthin' clanky-clank?' That's what you want me to say?"

"Or anything! Just be a trash-talking robot!"

"What's the script say?" he asked.

"There ain't no script!" I told him.

J.R. kept looking confused. "Ain't you gotta write a script first? Like you did last time?"

"No, man! This is improv! Just gotta improvise! Pretend you're the Hatebot 3000! Running up on Toothpick!"

"With a garbage can on my head?" he asked me.

"Yeah, man! Just run up to where that fast-food wrapper is—"

"How am I gonna see it?"

"You just look down! Wrapper's on the ground! You can peep it under the can! Soon as you get to the wrapper, stop and give me a couple headbutts. Then we'll tussle. And—BAM!—I'll karate-kick you. Then you stagger back outta frame. Feel me?"

J.R. looked at the garbage can. "I gotta wear this? On my head? And you're gonna kick me while I'm wearing it?"

"I ain't gonna kick you hard!" I said. "It's just a movie kick. It's mostly pretend."

"What part of the movie this gonna be?" he asked me.

"I dunno! Figure it out later."

"Do I gotta wear a garbage can for the whole movie?"

"Don't worry about that! There ain't a movie yet! It's just a teaser!"

"How you make a teaser for something that don't exist?"

"Man, will you quit with these questions? We're running out of daylight!"

J.R. shook his head and huffed out a sigh. "I don't know about this, fam."

Truth was, I didn't know, either. But I was desperate. I'd just checked my numbers, and I still only had 550 followers.

I was 450 short of monetizing!

"Please!" I begged J.R. "I need this! If I can monetize, I'll share the money with you!"

He shook his head again. But he picked up the can and moved over to where I'd told him to start. I turned back to where my phone was.

That's when I saw the little rug rat.

Couldn't have been more than three years old. Little dude had wandered over from the kiddie side of the playground. Had my phone in his hand. Fixin' to bite down on it like a sandwich!

"Get that phone out of your mouth, little dude! We're making a movie!"

"I thought it was a teaser!" J.R. yelled.

"He don't know what a teaser is!" I yelled back while I wrestled my phone from the little rug rat.

Aw, man! Now my phone had toddler drool all over it!

I started wiping it off on my leg. Little rug rat just stood there, looking at my phone like it was lunch.

Then his mama came over. Swooped him up.

"I'm so sorry," she said. "He's just at that age."

"It's all good," I said. "But we're shooting a movie here? So—"

"Thought it was a teaser!" J.R. yelled. I ignored him. Figured he was just trying to wind me up.

Rug rat's mom took him back to the kiddie side. I got my phone all set up again.

"You ready?" I asked J.R.

He picked up the garbage can. Looked into it. Screwed up his face. "You gonna owe me for this one, fam."

"Totally! For the rest of my life! And if we monetize, I'll pay you!"

J.R. liked the sound of that. Put the garbage can on his head. "CLANKETY-FILTH—"

"Wait!" I yelled. "Let me call action first!"

I pressed record on my phone. Then I ran into position.

As I was running, I realized something:

I had no clue what I was going to say for my OWN lines.

I stopped for a second. Trying to think it through.

"ARE WE GOING?" J.R. yelled from inside the can. His voice sounded all small and echoey.

"Not just yet! And yell louder!" I told him as I got into position. Struck a Toothpick super-pose. Then I counted down. "Three! Two! One! ACTION!"

J.R. started for me with the can on his head. "CLANKETY-FILTHY-CLANK-CLANK-FILTH!" he yelled.

"NOT TODAY, HATEBOT 3000!" I yelled back.

J.R. was having trouble running with a garbage can

on his head. Took him a lot longer than I expected to get to the fast-food wrapper where he was supposed to stop and fight me.

Then he blew right past it. Plowed into me. I just about fell over. But I had to stand my ground so I wouldn't get knocked out of frame.

I pushed him back. Then he went too far. Started losing his balance. So I had to reach out and grab the bottom lip of the garbage can. Kinda tug him back toward me so he'd stay in the shot.

I heard him mutter from under the can. "Man, whatchu—"

"TAKE THAT!" I yelled, trying to cover so my phone mic wouldn't pick up his muttering.

"You draggin' me—!"

"Shhhh!"

I got him back to where he needed to be. He steadied himself.

But then he just stood there.

"Come at me!" I hissed, hoping I was quiet enough that my phone wouldn't pick up the sound.

J.R. staggered forward. I leaned into him to make it look like he was headbutting me.

"CLANKY FILTH!" he yelled.

Then I gave him a kick. Knocked him back out of frame. He fell on his butt.

"OOOW!"

I turned to face the phone so I could spit my last lines right into the camera. The most important lines in the whole teaser!

That's when I saw the rug rat.

He was coming in from the left side. Trying to swoop back in on my phone.

I put my arms up in another super-pose and started running at the camera, hoping I'd scare him off while I yelled:

"*TOOTHPICK FIGHTS THE HATEBOT 3000!* COMING SOON!"

Little rug rat didn't get scared off. Just started toddling faster. Like he was racing me to my phone. Reaching his hand out for it, fixing to wreck my shot!

"SMASH THAT SUBSCRIBE BUTTON FOR MORE!" I yelled.

Couldn't tell if I got the line off before his stubby little fingers grabbed my phone and shoved it in his mouth.

By the time I got it back, my phone was dripping with rug-rat drool again.

His mom came over and scooped him up. "I'm so sorry!" she told me. But I was starting to think she wasn't THAT sorry. Or it wouldn't have happened twice.

Then J.R. limped over, rubbing his rear end. "Think I broke my butt, fam!"

I called it a wrap at that point.

Didn't have a choice. The sun was down, my battery was dead, and J.R.'s butt was broke.

## CHAPTER 16

# NO SLEEP TILL *HELEN*

Fact: I do not actually know how to make a movie.

Or even a teaser for a movie.

I know how to make parts of one. Like, I can act a role. Or write a screenplay. But when it comes to editing? Titles? Sound effects? Music? All that other stuff you need to turn a plain old video into something dope?

That ain't my thing. It's Sierra's thing.

So as soon as I came home and plugged my phone in, I texted her.

> I shot the teaser
> can u edit it?

Lol no

That's YOUR channel

I'm busy with MY channel

PLEASE????

Don't u want to monetize

Yes I do

MY channel

BTW Jazmin coming to my place at 6am to do makeup

Do u want to come too? We will film for collab

I don't need makeup!!!

U do u king. See u at 7

I couldn't believe that girl's attitude.

But I was on my own. Nothing to do but finish that teaser myself.

I got out Dad's laptop. Checked my MeTube numbers first. By now, it was impossible for me to go online and NOT check my numbers right away. I'd been doing it all day long.

They'd barely changed since the last time I'd looked.

Just over a million and a half views. Five hundred fifty-six subscribers.

Seeing that subscriber number was like a reverse Elektro zap. It brought me down!

If I wanted to hit a thousand, I NEEDED that teaser!

I opened up the movie-making app on Dad's laptop. It was one of those basic programs. Comes with the computer. Wasn't half as fancy as what Sierra uses when she edits. But it was all I had.

And it might've been basic. But it was NOT easy.

You ever open up a computer program you've never used before? And there's so many buttons and menus and sliders and statuses and whatnot that you just freak out? Feel like you're having a heart attack?

But you're all, "Gotta get it done!" So you upload your video file and just dive in? But none of the buttons on the program make any sense? And you click a button, thinking it'll do one thing? But it turns out it does a whole other thing? That you don't even really understand?

Then you can't figure out how to UN-do the thing you just did?

So you click a couple more buttons. Then the program throws up a question box like, "You sure you want to rewrite this file?"

And you're like, "Man, I don't know! DO I?"

Then all of a sudden, it's two hours later, and you're

beating your head against the kitchen table? 'Cause you can't figure out how to change the stupid font size on the titles? After you spent half an hour just trying to FIND the dumb titles in the menu options?

That's what it was like trying to make my own teaser. Nothing but pain.

By the time Dad came home with burritos for dinner, I was beat.

I had an okay-looking title on it by then. *Toothpick Fights the Hatebot 3000!* Used this retro-looking font. Like it was a classic comic.

But the rest of it was just trash. My footage was no good!

J.R. didn't look like any kind of robot. Just a kid with a garbage can on his head. Plus, we were too far from the camera. The light was all wrong. The fight seemed fake. And that little rug rat ruined everything! His big noggin-y head showed up right when I was yelling, "Smash that subscribe button!"

I couldn't cut the rug rat out without losing that last line. And it was the whole point of the teaser!

"You feeling okay?" Dad asked me when he sat down with the burritos. "You look kinda sick."

"It's my teaser, Dad! It's terrible!"

"I bet it isn't. Let me take a look at it."

I showed Dad the teaser. And I could tell just watching his face it was no good.

"See what I mean? It's trash, Dad!"

"The little shorty at the end is funny."

"It's not supposed to be funny! He ain't even supposed to be there!"

"Why you sweating this?" Dad asked me. "You got a great movie. What more do you need?"

"I need more content! So I can get a thousand subscribers! So I can monetize!"

Dad just shrugged. "Seems to me you'll get plenty of subscribers when folks see you on *Helen*. So the only thing you NEED . . . is a good night's sleep."

He wasn't wrong. I was wiped out. Soon as I finished dinner, I gave up on the trailer. Crawled off to bed.

But then I couldn't sleep!

You ever get too tired to sleep? 'Cause you're just THAT worn out?

Plus, you know once you wake up, a car's coming to drive you to the biggest talk show in the world?

That didn't help matters. I couldn't stop thinking about *The Helen Show*.

And I was getting some NERVES.

That feeling I'd had the day before, like I was up on a tall ladder, looking down and freaking out like I might fall? Man, it was ten times worse now.

What if I froze up and couldn't talk? On nationwide TV?

What if I looked a fool? In front of the whole world?

On my mama's favorite TV show?

What if she was looking down on me from heaven? And I let her down?

I conked out eventually. Had a bunch of weird dreams. Kept waking up.

All of a sudden, it was six-thirty. My alarm was beeping.

Time to get up and go!

But I felt TERRIBLE.

Bone-tired. Headache. Sour stomach.

First thing I did was check my numbers on MeTube. They were flat. Just two new subscribers.

Dad was making eggs in the kitchen. Smell of them made my stomach turn.

I took a hot shower. It helped a little. Not much.

Then I went to get dressed.

That's when the real trouble started.

"DAD! WHERE'S MY GOOD SHIRT?"

It was nowhere to be found! And I only had the one! Everything else in my drawer was T-shirts and sweats. I couldn't go on *The Helen Show* in a T-shirt!

Dad came into my bedroom. He was in a suit. Looked sharp!

Not me. I was in my underwear. Freaking out!

"WHERE'S MY SHIRT!"

"Settle down," he told me. "It's here. Shirts don't just walk away. Now, think back: Where'd you put it after you finished the laundry Sunday night?"

"OH, MAN!"

I never finished that laundry!

## CHAPTER 17

# ROLLING IN THE STRETCH . . . AND THE STENCH

Let me tell you about a thing called mildew.

It is a FUNGUS. And if you leave wet laundry shut up inside an old wash machine? In a dank, stinky basement? For a whole day and a half?

You'll get some serious mildew growing on that laundry. You can't really see it. But you can smell it.

That fungus smells FUNKY.

And now my only good shirt did, too!

There wasn't time to wash it again. The car was coming to pick us up!

So all Dad and I could do was put my shirt in the dryer with one of those fabric sheets. Supposed to make your laundry smell fresh.

"That'll get the stink out," Dad told me.

Then we ran back upstairs to eat breakfast. I didn't feel much like eating. But my butt was dragging, and Dad thought if I got some eggs in me, they'd give me energy.

So I forced down the eggs with a couple pieces of toast. Except the more I ate, the worse I felt!

Then I brushed my teeth while Dad went down and fetched my shirt from the dryer.

He came back up holding it out like a dead cat.

"It's a little ripe still," he said.

It was more than a little ripe. Smelled like moldy basement and rotten leaves.

"What am I gonna do, Dad?"

He shrugged. "You could wear a sweatshirt. Or your Toothpick shirt."

"But I gotta look sharp! You KNOW Sierra's gonna be dressed up."

"We could try to stop at a clothing store on the way," Dad said. "Except it's seven in the morning."

The car was coming any minute. I had to choose between looking good and smelling good.

And I figured, if I was going to be on TV? Folks can't smell you through the TV.

So I put the smelly shirt on.

That's when I started feeling like the Swamp Zombie.

Just smelling myself made my stomach want to go in reverse!

"Oh, man! I think those eggs might come back up."

"I'll bring a bag," Dad said. "Just in case."

We went out to the front stoop to wait for the car.

Then my nose started to stuff up. The same way it gets sometimes when I go downstairs to do laundry. Like I'm allergic to just being in that moldy old basement.

When I figured out what was happening, I started to freak out.

"Dad!"

"What's the matter, son?"

"I think I'm allergic to my shirt!"

He put his hand on my shoulder. "Want me to run up and get another one?"

"I don't HAVE another one!"

"Want to borrow one of mine?"

"You're three times my size!"

Then I saw the limo turn up our street.

And if I hadn't been sleepy, barfy, stuffy, smelly, and scared? I would've been hyped.

But it was just not a good situation.

Dad looked worried.

"You going to be okay?" he asked. "I can run up, get you a T-shirt."

The limo was coming to a stop in front of us. I took a deep breath. When I let it out, my lungs wheezed.

But I shook it off. "I'll be okay."

Dad gave my back a little rub. "Just let me know," he said. "I got your back."

Limo driver hopped out. Came around to hold the door open for us.

"Welcome aboard!" Dude was pretty cheerful for seven in the morning.

"Thank you, sir!" said Dad.

I thanked the dude, too, as I got in. Just praying I wouldn't pass out, or puke, or stop breathing in his limo. Didn't think his smile would hold up too long if any of that happened.

The back of that limo was huge! Tinted windows. Leather seats. Wood panels. Looked like a cross between a nightclub and a spaceship. There was a basket of snacks off to one side, sitting on top of a cabinet with a fridge underneath. I took the far seat, facing backward. Dad sat down next to me.

The limo started moving.

"How you doing?" Dad asked.

It was a tough question. On the one hand, I was riding in a limo!

And my nose was so stuffed up, I couldn't smell my shirt anymore. So that was actually a plus.

But there was some bad stuff going on in my belly. It was like a wrestling match down there! Felt like those eggs were jumping off the top rope of my stomach. Bashing that toast in a piledriver. And the toast was fixin' to come back with a facebuster.

"Can I get that bag?" I asked Dad.

He handed over the plastic bag he'd brought. I opened it up. Put it between my knees. Tried to breathe deep.

Dad leaned over and checked out the fridge. It was full of soda, juice, and water.

"You want some water?" he asked. "Might settle your stomach."

I shook my head. The stuffy nose was making me dizzy.

Dad patted me on the leg. "Hang in there. It'll pass."

Didn't seem like it was passing. All those eggs wanted to do was climb up out of my stomach.

I leaned over and stuck my head in the bag.

"Let it out if you have to," Dad told me.

I felt the limo stop. I was hoping we were just at a light. But then I heard the door open.

"We're getting in the limo now . . ." I heard Sierra say, almost like she was telling the story to somebody. Then she said, *Ohmygosh!* Marcus, are you okay?"

I didn't want to lift my head out of the bag to answer. All I could do was focus on not throwing up.

"We're having some challenges," I heard Dad tell her.

Then I heard Sierra's mom. "Good morning, Keith—*oh, dear!* Is he all right?"

"Morning, Jacqueline. It's a little touch and go at the moment."

I felt the limo start to move again. Made those eggs want to move, too.

"What's that *smell*?" I heard Sierra say.

"I don't smell anything," Dad said, all innocent-like. Trying to cover for me.

"You can't smell that? It's like something up and *died* in here."

"That so?" Dad asked. "Well, I can't imagine what that could be."

"It's my shirt!" I moaned.

"Oh, THAT," said Dad. "Yeah, we had a little laundry situation." Then he explained to them about the mildew.

"Marcus, honey, I am *so* sorry you're having such a hard time," Mrs. Martinez told me.

Then I heard her whisper to Sierra.

"Sweetheart, I think you should stop recording."

*RECORDING?*

My head shot up out of that bag. I saw Sierra and her mom for the first time. Sitting across from us.

They looked GOOD. Like they were going to church. And not just any church. A nice one! Stained glass windows and whatnot.

Sierra's hair was all done up. Looked like she had makeup on, too. And she was pointing her stupid phone right at me.

Like she was FILMING ME!

"WHAT YOU DOING?" I yelled at her.

"It's behind-the-scenes content," she told me. "For my MeTube channel."

"I GOT MY HEAD IN A BAG!"

Sierra's mom reached out and put a hand on Sierra's phone arm. "Put it down, honey. It's not appropriate."

"Heck, yeah, it's not appropriate!" I yelled at Sierra.

She huffed out a sigh and lowered the phone. "Sorry."

Didn't look sorry. And she still had that camera lens pointed at me!

I was fixin' to go full Wolf Boy on that girl.

But instead, what I did was barf up my breakfast.

## CHAPTER 18

# BACKSTAGE AT THE BIG SHOW

Ninety-nine percent of what I threw up went in the bag.

The other one percent was a problem. We had to stop at a gas station to clean up.

Cheerful driver was A LOT less cheerful after that. I felt bad for him. And also just bad in general.

After Dad bought me some seltzer water and breath mints, we got back on the road. My shirt was still stuffing up my nose, and I was pretty shaky. But at least there was nothing left in my belly to barf up.

"You can't post that stuff you shot," I told Sierra.

"It's great behind-the-scenes content," she said.

"I'm throwing up in a bag!"

"I know!" she said. "That's what makes it great content."

Mrs. Martinez was on my side. "Sweetheart, that's not right," she told Sierra. "You can't post any of that without Marcus's say-so."

I had to agree.

Then I fell asleep. For the whole rest of the trip.

Next thing I knew, Dad was shaking me awake.

"Marcus! We're here!"

The limo door was open. Sierra and her mom had already gotten out.

I was so out of it from being asleep, I felt like I was under water.

I followed Dad out the door. I was half thinking we'd step out of that limo onto some kind of red-carpet situation.

But it wasn't like that. We were outside this warehouse-looking building in a grimy part of town. Half a block away, there was a line of folks on the sidewalk. They must've been the audience, waiting to get in the studio.

When I stepped out, a couple of them perked up, thinking I might be famous.

Once they got a look at me, they UN-perked.

There was a woman waiting at the front door with a headset on, holding a clipboard. All sunshine and smiles.

"Hi there!" she said. "I'm Mindy! I'm your segment producer. We're SO excited you could join us! We love your movie SO MUCH!"

"Thank you!" Sierra said. Then she held up her phone. "Is it okay if I film this?" she asked Mindy. "For a *Behind the Scenes* vlog on my MeTube channel?"

"Ohmygosh, of course! What a great idea!" Mindy said.

It did NOT seem like a great idea to me. I was about to say something. But then Mindy wrinkled up her nose and gave the air a frowny sniff like, *Who farted?*

I figured she must have gotten a whiff of my funky fungus shirt. So I should just keep my mouth shut and not draw attention.

I don't know why I thought, *If I'm quiet enough, she can't smell my shirt.* But I was still pretty groggy from that nap. So I wasn't thinking straight.

After we all introduced ourselves, Mindy led us into the warehouse-looking studio building. Inside, there was a big hallway that led to what I guess was the stage. But we didn't go that direction. Instead, Mindy took us through an unmarked door to a part of the building that was mostly offices, with people coming in and out.

A couple of them stopped to say hi. One was Chad, the

dude who DM'd us. Mindy said he was the "talent coordinator." Which I guess is another way of saying, "The dude who DMs you when they want you to come on the show."

Chad wrinkled his nose, too. That got me feeling like a Swamp Zombie again. Like I was stuck in that one issue of the comic where the Swamp Zombie tries to go to a grocery store. And everybody runs away from him, like *iiiick!*

It didn't feel too good, thinking I was the *ick* in this situation.

Sierra was still filming everything on her phone. I didn't feel too good about that, either.

Mindy took us down a hallway to our dressing room. It had a couch with a coffee table and some nice chairs, plus a mirror and a countertop along one wall.

There was a plate of breakfast pastries and fruit on the counter, along with some water bottles. On the coffee table was a big bowl full of bite-size candy bars. They were a brand I'd never heard of: Choköbjär!

"Have you tried Choköbjärs?" Mindy asked me when she caught me staring at them. "They're SO good! Helen discovered them when she was in Europe on vacation. We're all hooked now!"

"Look at *this*!" Sierra said. She was over at the countertop. Next to the plate of food were two shiny gift bags. One of them had Sierra's name on it. The other one had mine.

Those bags were BIG. I was thinking, *You could fit a horse in that bag! Did Helen buy us a horse?*

Then Sierra reached into hers and pulled out this huge fluffy white bathrobe with the *Helen Show* logo on the chest.

"Oh, my!" Sierra's mom said.

"We get to keep these?" Sierra asked.

"Of course!" Mindy told her. "There's a coffee mug in there, too. If the robe's the wrong size, just let us know. We'll swap it out."

"I should reshoot this," Sierra said. "Make it an UNBOXING video!" She folded the bathrobe up and put it back in the bag. Started plotting with her mom about how to shoot herself pretending to open her gift bag robe for the first time.

Whole thing made me roll my eyes.

Meanwhile, Dad had taken Mindy aside for a chat.

"Is there a store nearby where I can get Marcus a new shirt?" he asked. "We had a little laundry incident. The one he's wearing caught some mildew."

"Ooooh." Mindy's eyes got all wide, and she nodded. Like all of a sudden, the stink was making sense to her. "That might be a good idea! There's a department store about ten blocks east of here. But I'm not sure if you can make the timing work. It's only about forty minutes until the kids tape their segment."

"I'll make it!" Dad said. Before I knew it, he was sprinting out the door to buy me a new shirt.

Then Mindy left the room, saying she'd leave us to get settled. And when she came back, we'd do a "pre-interview." Whatever that meant.

So I was left alone with Sierra, her mom, and their stupid gift-bag-bathrobe-unboxing video business.

I didn't want any part of it. So while they fussed over Sierra and the gift bag, I ate some pastries from the plate. They were delicious. But I was starving by then. I could've eaten cardboard and been happy about it.

Then I moved on to that big bowl of Choköbjärs.

And let me tell you something about those Choköbjärs: They were GJÖÖD!

I ate six. Which was probably about five too many. Because between them and the pastries, I could feel myself getting some serious sugar shakes.

Then Sierra tried to drag me into her *Behind the Scenes* vlog nonsense.

"Let's shoot some content!" she told me.

"Heck, no!"

"C'mon! Just do one with me!"

She nodded to her mom, who hit record. Sierra stood next to me and talked into the camera with this extra-cheerful, fake-TV-host voice that was way too loud:

"Hello, hello, hello! Welcome back to the *Sierra Cinematic Universe!*"

"The what now?" I asked. But she just kept going.

"Your home for quality comedy entertainment twenty-four-seven, three-sixty-five! We're backstage at *The Helen Show* with the one, the only, the LEGENDARY Marcus Jenkins, aka Puffer from *Phone Zombies*—keep an eye out for episode two, dropping any minute now on the *SCU!*"

"The SC-WHAT?"

Sierra turned toward me, but she didn't take her eyes off the phone her mama was holding up to record us. So it was like she was talking to the camera instead of me.

"The *SCU!* The *Sierra Cinematic Universe!*"

"Girl, what are you even talking about?"

Sierra smirked into the camera. Gave it a wink. "He's a little slow," she said. "But he'll get there."

Oh, man.

OH, MAN.

Remember how I said when somebody pushes my

buttons, I can get so mad, I turn into Wolf Boy? When that happens, it's usually 'cause somebody's been clowning me. Trying to make me look small. That HURTS. A LOT. And somehow, my brain turns the hurt into mad.

And that's on a good day.

This was not a good day. 'Cause I hadn't slept more than a couple hours the last two nights. I had the full-on sugar shakes. I was scared out of my head about messing up on *The Helen Show*. I'd just barfed in my first-ever limo. And there was a fungus crawling all over me!

Then Sierra wanted to stick a camera in my face and call me SLOW?

Well, that was a guaranteed Wolf Boy situation.

"I AIN'T PLAYING THIS!" I yelled. "TURN THAT CAMERA OFF!"

It came out so loud, Sierra took a quick step away from me. Like Wolf Boy was fixin' to bite her head off.

Sierra's mom came down on my side. She lowered the phone. Stopped recording. Gave her daughter a LOOK.

"Sierra!" she snapped. "That is out of line!"

"I'm just goofing!" Sierra said.

"That was NOT goofing," Mrs. Martinez told her. "It was just cruel!"

I was starting to get emotional. Like actual tears were building up in me.

Which was confusing! Sierra's mom was sticking up for me! But that almost made me feel worse.

"I'm sorry, Marcus," Sierra told me.

I couldn't tell if she meant it or not. I couldn't tell up from down just then. My brains were scrambled.

Why the heck was my body trying to CRY?

That's when Mindy came back in the room. All smiles.

"Ready for the pre-interview?"

## CHAPTER 19

# TEN MINUTES TILL SHOWTIME!

I guess they call it a pre-interview 'cause when she does it, Mindy PRE-tends to be Helen.

She sat us down on the dressing room couch. Told us how the interview would go. What questions Helen would ask. That kind of thing.

I tried to listen. But I was too busy trying to unscramble my brains. Plus, I was worried about Mindy smelling my stinky shirt. What if Helen smelled it on TV?

Wolf Boy was long gone by now. I was back to being Swamp Zombie. Stinky, scared, sleepy, and sugar-shaky all at once.

So it was not easy to focus on whatever Mindy was telling us.

Until I clocked her saying, "Then after that, Tevin will join us."

I just about jumped off the couch. "Tevin BART's gonna be here?"

Mindy and Sierra just kinda looked at me.

"Were you listening, Marcus?"

"Maybe," I said. "Can you run it by me again?"

"Tevin's filming a movie in Budapest right now," Mindy told me. "But he's going to join us by satellite to talk about how he discovered your movie online."

"DOPE!" I said.

"I know, right?" said Mindy. "Then after that, Marcus— we thought it'd be nice if Helen asked you about why you dedicated the movie to your mother."

When I heard that, my stomach started flipping. And my face got hot.

"Can we not talk about that?" I asked Mindy.

"But it's so touching!" she told me.

"It's a little TOO touching," I said.

That was true. The thing is, sometimes when people talk about my mom, it doesn't bug me at all. But other times, I get emotional. And I had ALREADY almost cried today for no good reason.

So I was afraid if Helen started asking me about my mom? That could start some real waterworks.

And I did NOT want to go crying on national TV.

"Are you sure?" Mindy asked again.

I nodded. "Please don't talk about that."

Mindy made a sad face. But she said okay.

Then she started saying some other stuff. I couldn't really focus on it. 'Cause on top of everything else, now I had to worry about crying on TV!

That scared feeling in my stomach was back. The one where I felt like I was about to fall off a fifty-foot ladder.

I took a deep breath. Filled my chest up with air.

But my lungs were all wheezy from being allergic to my shirt. So when I let it out, I made this *huuuggggh* noise.

Mindy and Sierra both looked at me like I was some kind of freak.

"Are you okay?" Mindy asked.

"I'm good," I said.

Although that was not exactly true.

Then some big, bald dude wearing a headset poked his head in the door and yelled, "TEN MINUTES!"

Mindy jumped right up. "Oh my goodness!" she said. "We've got to get you into makeup."

*Makeup?*

Oh, man!


Mindy took us down the hallway to a whole other room. There were four chairs set up in front of a mirror. Two makeup artist women were waiting there, like barbers in a shop. They put Sierra and me into chairs.

My makeup woman was even more friendly than Mindy. "Good morning!" she said. "I'm Tyra!"

"I'm Marcus," I told her.

Then I saw her nose wrinkle up.

"My shirt has mildew on it," I said.

She gave me a smile. "It's all good! We can work with that." She put a hand on my shoulder. "You are a very handsome young man, Marcus. And I am going to make you even MORE handsome."

Then she looked a little closer at my face. Kinda frowned. "Did you not get a whole lot of sleep last night?"

"Can you tell?" I asked her.

"Not when I'm through with you, honey."

Then she went to work on my face. Started using some kind of brush on the bags under my eyes. I tried to watch in the mirror.

"Is it going to look like I got makeup on?" I asked.

"Not at all, sweetheart," Tyra told me. "I'm a professional."

Then Sierra's makeup lady piped up from the next station over. "I'll tell you who ELSE is a professional—whoever did the first round on Sierra here."

"That's my girl, Jazmin," Sierra explained. "She came over to my place this morning and did my makeup for a collab. We both have MeTube channels. Hers is called *Jazmin Stylez*. It's a hair and makeup vlog."

"Well, you tell that Jazmin she's got a real future in this business," Sierra's makeup lady said.

Sierra looked in the mirror at her mama, who was standing behind her. "Can we get that on film?"

Mrs. Martinez shook her head. "We're not shooting anything else unless Marcus says it's okay."

Sierra looked at me. "Please?" she begged. "We'll keep you out of it. I won't say anything. I promise! And I'm sorry about clowning on you before. I know that wasn't cool."

The thing about Sierra is, when she *wants* to be nice? She can talk you into anything. And I didn't want any more drama. I was too busy trying to take deep breaths and calm myself down without sounding like a busted air conditioner.

So I said it was okay to shoot more as long as she kept me out of it.

Her makeup lady said yes, too. So Mrs. Martinez filmed a bit where the makeup lady gave Jazmin props again and Sierra talked into the camera in her extra-cheerful, fake-TV-host voice.

"You heard it here first! The *Jazmin Stylez* makeup game gets *The Helen Show*'s professional seal of approval! And don't sleep on the collabs we've got coming up between

*Jazmin Stylez* and the *Sierra Cinematic Universe*! Check your feed! More good stuff coming!"

I didn't see how Sierra could be using the same name for her MeTube channel that Capital Comics used for their movies. But I didn't want to say anything while her mama was filming.

Plus, Tyra was sweeping her brush all over my face. And I was worried if I opened my trap, I'd get a mouthful of makeup. So I kept it shut.

Finally, Tyra finished up. "You are good to go, baby!" she said.

I checked myself out in the mirror. Couldn't see much that was different.

Then the big, bald dude with the headset threw the door open. Yelled, "TWO MINUTES! KIDS TO THE STAGE!"

Mindy hustled us up and out of the makeup room. My heart was thumping about ten times normal speed.

I was just starting to worry Dad was about to miss the whole thing when we turned a corner and I saw him running up the hallway toward us. Sweating bullets in his suit and holding a shopping bag like it was a football.

"Hold the phone! New shirt coming!"

Did I mention I got the greatest dad in the world?

He'd bought me a dope-looking blue button-down in just the right size. Bit the tag off with his teeth and got it on me in record time.

"Thank you, Dad!"

He gave me a quick hug. Still breathing hard from his run across town. "It's all good. Break a leg out there! Not for real. It's just a thing people say."

"I know that," I told him.

"Ready to go?" Mindy asked.

I nodded. Then she led us through a big double door to the backstage area. All sorts of ropes and lights and furniture and whatnot were lying around. It was dark enough that I had to squint to see everything.

And it was COLD! Felt like it was about fifty degrees back there. Made me want to shiver.

Up ahead, there were some curtains. Through a break in them, I could see the stage. They must not have been shooting, because Helen was talking to some lady with a headset.

Then another dude with a headset met us. Took us over to stand by the break in the curtains.

While some other lady clipped a couple of tiny microphones to us, the dude with the headset started pointing out the furniture on stage.

"When we give the signal," he said, "you'll walk out and sit in those two chairs. Make sure you don't bump into that table on your way. And when Helen starts to interview Tevin Bart, DON'T LOOK BEHIND YOU. Watch him on the small monitors under those cameras right in front of you. Got it?"

I hoped I had it. My heart was going like a jackhammer.

I was SO SCARED.

Like I wasn't looking down from a fifty-foot ladder anymore. It was a thousand-foot ladder now. And I was fixin' to fall off and go *splat* all over the ground.

There was a bank of TV screens right behind the curtain on our side. Each one was showing the feed from one of the stage cameras.

*"BACK IN FIVE . . . FOUR . . . THREE . . ."*

Then we were watching Helen on one of the monitors as she introduced us. It was weird, 'cause out of the corner of my eye, I could ALSO see her in real life, from a whole different angle.

I was getting dizzy. Felt like I was in a dream or something.

*"Our next guests are two filmmakers you've probably never heard of . . . but I've got a feeling that won't be the case for long. Let's take a look at some of their work."*

Then one of the monitors switched to playing clips from *Toothpick Fights the Doom!*

They'd spliced together bits and pieces of three different scenes:

First one was the scene where Darren, our film class teacher, is playing Prince Ka. He's dying on the sidewalk next to my bus stop. I find him there, and he gives me the magic toothpick. Then he croaks, and his body disappears. Which freaks me out. Then I get on the bus. When it pulls away, we see Tyrell standing there dressed as the Doom. Amari's soundtrack gives it a big *DUN-DA-DUN!* to make it dramatic.

Second scene was me on the city bus, getting freaked out when Sierra as Genie appears out of nowhere and tells me the toothpick will give me superpowers. And I have to save the universe from the Doom. I freak out even more when she says that. It's a pretty funny scene.

Third one they showed was me and Tyrell going at it in the big fight at the end of the movie. That's always a gut-buster.

Watching those scenes took me back. I got that good feeling I always get when I think about how hard it was to make the movie. And how good it turned out for all the work we did.

The studio audience was LOVING it! Every time we got to a punch line, they ROARED with laughter.

Each one of those laughs gave me a big old Elektro jolt of energy.

And each time I got that Elektro jolt, I felt a little less scared.

Like maybe this was all gonna work out okay after all.

Then I heard Helen's voice.

*"Please welcome future Academy Award winners Marcus Jenkins and Sierra Martinez!"*

"GO! GO! GO!" yelled the headset dude.

Applause from the studio audience was ringing in my ears. Headset dude was pointing us toward the stage.

I followed Sierra into the bright lights.

# CHAPTER 20

# THE BIGGEST FIVE MINUTES OF MY LIFE

First thing I did was bump into the table. Same one the headset dude had warned me not to bump into.

Audience was clapping and whooping. And when I almost tripped over the table, they laughed.

It sounded like a bad laugh. Like they were laughing AT me. My face got hot. I was feeling dizzy.

Found my way to the chair I was supposed to sit in, next to Sierra. Across from Helen.

It was the first time I'd ever seen a famous person up close.

And you know what?

She looked even MORE famous in person than on TV.

Partly, it was her clothes. She had a pantsuit on. Nicest pantsuit I ever saw in my life. Made out of silk or something! Looked like a queen!

The Queen of Pantsuits!

Then I checked out the audience. Lights were shining in my eyes so bright, I almost couldn't see them. But there were A LOT of folks. Mostly ladies. Every one of them staring at us!

My head was spinning. Heart racing. Stomach turning.

Then I realized Helen was talking. And I should probably be listening.

"So how did this all come about?" she was asking.

"It was a real group effort," Sierra told her. "And I want to say, first and foremost, all thanks and glory be to God for blessing this project and everyone who worked on it. Shoutout to our whole amazing cast and crew: Jazmin Baptiste, Amari Simpson, Khalid El-Mazri, Tyrell Witherspoon, Antonio Sylvester, Ivan Nuñez, Dalan Davis—"

When Sierra said those last three names, I was thinking, *Who even ARE these people?*

Then I realized she was talking about Sly, Naz, and Double D! They had actual real names! *How did Sierra even know that?*

She was still finishing up her list of thanks:

"And finally, an extra-special thank-you shout-out to Darren Bode and Trish Stevens, our fantastic film teachers from the Afternoon Adventures program."

The audience gave Sierra a big round of applause. Then Helen fixed the crowd with a big old grin and said, "Why do I have the feeling we'll be hearing that speech at the Oscars in a few years?"

That got a whole OTHER round of applause.

"I don't know about that," said Sierra. "I just want to work hard and do my best to create good stories that people enjoy."

Man, you couldn't stop the applause after that. Sierra sat there grinning, soaking it up. And I started thinking, *How come she's doing all the talking?*

*Why aren't I talking?*

*Should I be talking?*

Applause was starting to slow.

*Was I supposed to say something now?*

*Oh, man! What am I supposed to say?*

"I work hard, too," I said.

That got a BIG laugh.

But it felt like the wrong kind again.

My face got even hotter. My heart beat even faster.

Felt like I was falling through the air! About to go *splat* on the ground!

*How do I stop it?*

Helen grinned at me. "I bet you DO work hard!"

"I want to thank everybody, too!" I said. "All those, um, y'know, like, shout-out to—uh, those—the, um, same people Sierra just said. Especially the—with the—names I didn't—everybody! Across the board! Also God. And Jesus! And my dad. He's backstage. Just brought me a—see, 'cause I needed—well, 'cause I forgot—that's a long—it's, like— uhh—never mind."

I did NOT mean to run my mouth like that. It's just that once I got started, I didn't know how to stop! Might have been all those Choköbjärs in my system.

There were some giggles in the crowd. Then Helen said, "Oh, my. That was a lot of words."

She got a BIG laugh for that. And it was DEFINITELY the wrong kind.

I was just in free fall by then. My head was spinning so hard, I got to thinking I might pass out.

Helen was saying some stuff. I didn't even know what.

I started to shiver. It was so cold in there!

Then all of a sudden, Tevin Bart was on the monitors. Talking about US!

"I was blown away by the creativity of these kids!" he was saying. "And the joy they brought to their filmmaking!

Also, the CRAFT of it. We were talking about this on set yesterday—some of the shot compositions these kids pulled off were next level. . . ."

I didn't know what Tevin Bart was even talking about. Like, what even WAS "shot composition"?

But Sierra was grinning like her face might fall off.

Then before I knew it, Tevin Bart was gone from the monitors. And Helen was asking, "So what's next for you two?"

"Well, for me personally," Sierra said, "I've just launched my new MeTube channel. The *Sierra Cinematic Universe*. It's quality comedy entertainment, twenty-four-seven, three-sixty-five. Our first limited series just premiered.

It's called *Phone Zombies*. It's a horror comedy about an evil smartphone app that enslaves our whole school."

"That sounds fantastic!" said Helen. "It's a horror comedy, you say?"

"It is," Sierra told her. "Because this modern technology, y'know, a lot of us are addicted to our phones. And that is scary! But if it's not YOU who's addicted? It can be funny, too."

"It really is," said Helen. "You know, our director, Bob, is addicted to HIS phone."

She pointed to a short dude standing next to one of the cameras. The dude nodded like he was busted, and everybody laughed.

"Is it affecting his work?" Sierra asked. Everybody laughed some more.

Then they started going back and forth about this dude Bob and his phone. Folks were just eating it up. Helen, Sierra, Bob, the audience. Having a grand old time!

Everybody except me. I was just sitting there like a fool.

And I was starting to get mad. Sierra was taking up all the space! Like I wasn't even there!

"So this *Phone Zombies* series, it's on YOUR channel?" Helen asked Sierra.

"Yes. That's the *Sierra Cinematic Universe*. S-I-E-R-R-A—"

"She's gonna get sued for that name," I said.

Audience laughed at that. BIG laugh.

Not only that? It was a GOOD laugh. For the first time, they were laughing WITH me!

Got a big boost of Elektro energy from that!

Sierra was giving me side-eye. But Helen was laughing. "You think the name might cause Sierra some legal trouble?" she asked me.

"I think so," I said. "'Cause she just ripped it off from Capital Comics. And they don't play."

Got a few chuckles for that one. Somebody in the crowd even gave me a "Whooop!"

"Now, Marcus—do you have a MeTube channel of your own?" Helen asked.

"Yes, I do!" I told her. "It's the *Toothpick Superhero* channel."

"And that's where we can watch this whole movie that just went viral?"

I figured if Sierra was going to push her channel, I should push mine, too. So I went all in.

I said, "That's right, Helen! It's the ONLY place you can watch it! *Toothpick Superhero* channel's your home for all-new, original Toothpick content! Twenty-four whatever! Seven days a week! Year-round! Quality superhero action! Adventure! Villains! Fights! We got it all!"

I was running my mouth again. But this time, the crowd was into it. They were cheering me!

ZAP! Got another shot of Elektro energy. Straight to my brain!

So I kept going.

"And we're making a SEQUEL, Helen!"

Helen gave me a big old smile. "That sounds great! Tell me about it!"

"It's called *Toothpick Fights the Hatebot 3000!* Got a robot supervillain this time! Gonna be dope! Teaser's dropping on my channel TONIGHT!"

I was flying now. Practically coming out of my chair. Crowd was feeding on my Elektro energy! Whooping it up!

"Just so we're clear," Sierra piped up, "I was NOT involved with the making of that teaser."

The way she said it was ice-cold.

Crowd went *oooooh!*

I wasn't going to take that. So I fired right back:

"'Cause she don't know what's good!" I told Helen. "Her channel's just a bunch of dumb vlogs."

Got another big *oooooh!* Crowd was into it! Like they were watching a prize fight!

Helen sat back in her chair. Made her eyes all big. "Sounds like the two of you are having some creative differences."

"The trouble is, Helen," Sierra told her in a snotty voice, "that one of us is a little bit of a primo donut."

Crowd gave her the biggest *ooooh!* yet.

I could feel the whole studio looking at me. Like, *How's he going to clap back?*

And I was a little off my game for a second. Because until that moment, I had never in my life heard the words "primo donut" put together like that.

But the way it sounded to me, Sierra was saying a primo donut was the best thing ever. And SHE was it.

So I sat up in my chair and said, "That's ME! I'M the primo donut!"

Got a HUGE laugh for that!

POW! ZAP! I was riding high on that Elektro energy!

Sierra was staring at me like she couldn't believe what I was saying.

So I decided to stick the knife in. Double down! Get even more of that love from the crowd!

I said, "I'm a triple-glazed, jelly-filled, frosted-up, sprinkles-on-top, fresh-out-the-OVEN primo donut!"

Whole studio blew up. Everybody! Not just the crowd. Helen was roaring! That dude Bob was crying with laughter! All the folks in headsets! Everybody!

Even Sierra was laughing.

Which didn't make any sense. 'Cause I'd just owned that girl!

At least, that's what I was thinking.

Until I got off stage.

And I found out what "primo donut" meant.

## CHAPTER 21

# THE PRIMO DONUT

Turns out what Sierra said was NOT "primo donut."

It was *"prima donna."*

Which is not even English. It's Italian.

And what it means in Italian . . . is "BIG JERK."

So what happened was, Sierra called me a big jerk on national TV.

Then I called MYSELF a big jerk on national TV.

And I acted like I was proud of it!

'Cause Sierra had tricked me! With her stupid know-it-all Italian words!

When we got back to the dressing room, and I found out how she'd played me?

We had another Wolf Boy situation. It got out of hand for a minute. Our parents had to separate us. Mrs. Martinez dragged Sierra into the hallway for a talking-to, while Dad gave me the same treatment next to the fluffy bathrobe bags.

"I know it went a little off the rails out there," he told me. "But that girl is your FRIEND."

"She ain't acting like it!"

"You ain't, either, son!" Dad gave me a look like he wasn't kidding around.

"She made me look a fool! On TV!"

"No, it was good. Folks were laughing."

"Laughing AT me! Clowning on me!"

Dad took an extra half second before he answered. Like he was trying to decide whether or not to agree with what I'd said.

"It was fine! No such thing as bad publicity."

My stomach dropped halfway to my shoes when I heard that. "Why you calling it BAD?"

"I didn't mean it that way!"

I was feeling panicky. Sucked in my breath. Lowered my voice. "Tell me the truth, Dad. How bad was it?"

He took another beat before he answered. And my stomach hit the floor.

"It was FUNNY," he said. "That audience ate it up!"

"But they were laughing AT me! Did I screw up? Did I make a fool of myself?"

"No! It was fine!" Dad said for the third time.

But fine didn't mean good.

I was in full panic. Like I'd just made the biggest mistake of my life.

"Am I gonna be a goat? Is the whole world gonna laugh at me?"

"No, son! Really! Folks were eating it up! And they won't make you look bad when it airs on TV tomorrow. That's not how *The Helen Show* rolls. They're all about positivity. Now, c'mon. Let's get on home. Soon as you apologize to Sierra."

"What do I gotta apologize for?"

"Yelling at her on TV!"

"It was her fault!"

"Takes two to have an argument, son."

———

I told Sierra I was sorry. But I didn't mean it.

She told me she was sorry, too. But I could tell she didn't mean it, either.

It was just what we had to say to get our parents off our backs.

Before we left, I ate another pastry and some of the fruit plate. Would've dug back into those Choköbjärs, but the bowl was empty.

Then Mindy hustled us out of the dressing room. She said they were filming three shows that day, and they needed it for other guests.

Before I knew it, we were in the limo again, heading home.

"When we get back, do you want to work on a collab?" Sierra asked me. "So we can cross-promote *Phone Zombies* and that Toothpick teaser of yours?"

Oh, man!

I forgot all about that teaser!

I'd just told the whole world I was putting it online!

What was I gonna do?

I couldn't ask Sierra for help. I didn't even want to TALK to that girl. Let alone work on a whole trailer with her.

She probably wouldn't help me anyway. Just wanted to shoot more of those dumb vlogs.

I shook my head at her from across the limo. "I'm good," I said.

She and her mom traded looks. I got the feeling Sierra had only asked about a collab 'cause her mama told her to.

Then she shrugged. Said "Okay." Took out her phone and got to staring at it.

I was too tired to even look at my phone. It was out of charge anyway. I turned my big fluffy *Helen Show* bathrobe into a pillow and conked right out.

Didn't wake up again until we were stopped in front of Sierra's building.

Everybody was saying their goodbyes.

"Y'all enjoy the rest of your day now," Dad told them.

"You do the same!" said Mrs. Martinez.

Before she got out of the limo, Sierra asked me, "You sure you don't want to collab?"

"I'm good," I told her again.

But I wasn't good. I was bone-tired. Half-starving. And sick to my stomach over how bad I'd clowned myself with that primo donut nonsense.

Dad kept saying it was gonna be fine. But I didn't believe it. I was feeling like Swamp Zombie. And I didn't even smell bad anymore!

When we got home, it was afternoon. Dad fixed us some sandwiches for lunch. Then he went down to rerun the laundry with some bleach to get the mildew stink out of the load I'd messed up.

While he was gone, I got his laptop out. Checked my MeTube channel. Page views still around a million five. Subscriber number still flat at 558.

How many more did I need to monetize?

I plugged the numbers into the calculator on Dad's computer.

Needed 442 more subscribers.

I knew I'd get a lot more once *The Helen Show* aired. I just didn't know how many.

Sure would be sweet if I could get to a thousand. Not even for the money. Just so I could show up Sierra! Prove my movie was better than her dumb vlogs!

I clicked over to check out her channel. She'd done a whole makeover on it. Had this new "SIERRA CINEMATIC UNIVERSE" banner art.

It looked okay. But I could've done a much better job with the art. She should've asked me for help!

None of those vlogs she'd been shooting were posted yet. And she'd taken down all her older stuff. Like the full *Phone Zombies* movie that used to be there.

Her whole channel had just one video. It was called *PHONE ZOMBIES EPISODE ONE: CALM BEFORE THE STORM!*

I watched it. Turned out to be the first few minutes of the movie, with some new titles added to it. It was a good clip. No question. I was the costar, and I'd gotten some big laughs at the screening.

But it only had twelve page views! That was nothing! *Toothpick Fights the Doom!* had one and a half MILLION!

I was crushing her! No wonder that girl wanted to collab with me. Trying to steal my audience!

And if I could monetize? That'd really stick it to her. She'd be so jealous!

But I needed more content.

Like my teaser.

Did it really stink?

I opened up the file and rewatched it.

And I mean . . .

It wasn't perfect. Far from it.

Wasn't anywhere near as good as *Toothpick Fights the Doom!*

But it was all I had.

Dad came back upstairs. I asked him if he'd watch the

teaser again. Then I watched his face while he sat in front of the laptop.

He mostly looked blank. Right up until the end, when the little rug rat shows up and reaches for the phone while I'm yelling "SMASH THAT SUBSCRIBE BUTTON!"

Dad gave it a chuckle. "I still love that little shorty at the end."

"Is it good enough to post?" I asked him.

"I dunno," he said. "What do you think?"

"I think I just told the whole world I was putting a teaser out! So when people watch *The Helen Show*, they'll come looking for it. I gotta put it up!"

Dad gave me a shoulder shrug. "So put it up." Then he squinted his eyes at me. "Are you feeling okay?"

"I dunno." Truth was, I felt about six different kinds of bad. That nap in the limo had just made me even hungrier for some real sleep.

"You're looking pretty worn out," Dad said. "Why don't you finish that sandwich and go lie down for a bit? I'll head out to the market, get us something healthy for dinner."

After I finished my sandwich, I took off my good clothes and put on my new *Helen Show* robe. It was about three sizes too big. But it was so soft and fluffy, I felt like a millionaire in it.

I stretched out on the couch with Dad's laptop on my chest. Trying to decide whether to post the teaser on my channel.

I HAD to!

Didn't I? I'd told everybody on TV I would!

Maybe it wasn't even that bad.

The little rug rat was funny. Dad even said so.

And if I put it out . . . got a bunch of page views . . . maybe I could even get to a thousand subscribers BEFORE *The Helen Show* dropped! Set myself up to be making money on all the new clicks I'd get when the episode aired!

That'd show Sierra. I'd run circles around her dumb channel! No matter how much she'd hyped it on *Helen*!

I got another sick feeling in my stomach thinking about how I'd clowned myself with the primo donut business. But I shook it off.

That crowd was into me, man! I was making them laugh!

Heck, they might even love this teaser!

So I posted it. Put it right up on my page.

Then I took down the shout-out vlogs for Jazmin and Amari. Took down Khalid's stop-motion, too. Heck with those kids! They bailed on me! Wouldn't help me with the teaser when I needed it!

Now there were just two vids on my channel. The original movie and the teaser for *Toothpick Fights the Hatebot 3000!*

Which had zero views.

That couldn't be right! I hit refresh on my browser.

Still zero views.

Aw, man! That was even worse than Sierra's numbers!

Nobody was watching my teaser!

How could I get that number up?

Maybe I could get Tevin Bart to share it again.

Yeah! That was it! Dude loved me, man! He said so on *The Helen Show*!

I went on ClickChat to hit him up. Couldn't message him, 'cause his DMs are only open to people he follows. And he didn't follow me.

So instead, I bombed the comments on his latest post. Just straight-up BEGGING him to share my teaser:

**@marcusjenkns215** Yo Tevin its Marcus from the Helen Show

**@marcusjenkns215** Plz share my teaser for the Toothpick sequel!!

**@marcusjenkns215** Its on MeTube same page u shared the movie

**@marcusjenkns215** This is Marcus Jenkins

**@marcusjenkns215** U know how we are!

**@marcusjenkns215** PLZ SHARE THE TEASER W UR FANS

**@marcusjenkns215** I NEED UR HELP

**@marcusjenkns215** HMUUUUUUUUUUUU LEK:JWOIEFW

That last line I wrote? That's what happens when you fall asleep in the middle of writing a ClickChat comment.

## CHAPTER 22

# LATE-NIGHT STRAIGHT TALK

Next thing I knew, it was three in the morning. I woke up in my bed. Dad must've carried me there from the couch. I was so wiped out, I didn't even notice.

Turns out if you don't sleep much for a couple days, and then you DO sleep? You'll be out for a while. I think I must've clocked a good twelve hours.

First thing I did when I woke up was check my MeTube channel.

Teaser had about seven hundred views.

And . . . oh, man! I'd LOST ten subscribers!

How was that even possible?

I went over to ClickChat to beg Tevin Bart again in his comments. That's when I saw the notification:

**@tevinbart4real is following you**

Tevin Bart was following ME!

That meant I could DM him! Do my begging direct at the source!

So that's what I did. I started DM'ing him:

TEVIN ITS MARCUS

FROM THE HELEN SHOW

CAN U SHARE MY TEASER??? 🙏🙏🙏

PLEASE I NEED HELP GETTIN SUBSCRIBERS

SO I CAN MONETIZE!!!

I figured there was no chance he'd answer. It was three in the morning!

But I'd forgotten he was filming a movie in Europe someplace. So he was in a whole other time zone. (Probably eating some Choköbjärs, too.)

Ten seconds later, HE ANSWERED ME!

This is what he wrote:

> Hey champ

> U don't want me to share that video

*What?!* That didn't make any kind of sense. So I DM'd back:

> YES I DO!!!

Then he wrote:

> Trust me u don't

> Fact u might want to take it down

> It's 💩 💩 💩

OH, MAN! Tevin Bart called my teaser "poop emoji"! That HURT!

I was fixin' to type "OUCH" when he went on a whole DM run:

> But that's ok!!!

> When ur a creator, sometimes u miss the mark

> We all strike out sometimes

> I do too

> I've made some serious 💩 💩 💩 in my career

> Like Brain Police 2

I had to agree with Tevin Bart there. I'd seen *Brain Police 2*. It was nowhere near as good as the first *Brain Police*.

Then he asked me:

> U know why it was 💩 💩 💩?

> Cause we were doing it for the 💰 💰 💰

> And when u do it for the 💰 💰 💰 . . .

It's NEVER as good as when u do it for the 🖤 🖤 🖤

That's why ur Toothpick movie was so DOPE!

Cause u could see the 🖤 🖤 🖤 on the screen

And the 💪 💪 💪 too

That's what made it so 😂 😂 😂

This teaser doesn't have that yet

But u will get there

I BELIEVE IN U!!!

Just take your time. Put in the 💪 💪 💪 And the 🖤 🖤 🖤

And it will be GREAT!

U r a 💯 💯 💯 TALENT

Just don't go chasing that 💰 💰 💰

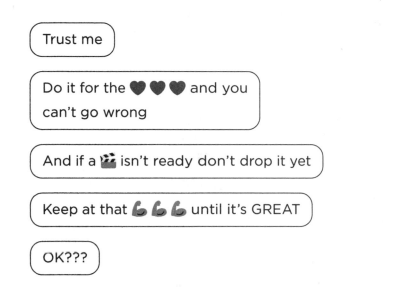

Trust me

Do it for the ♥ ♥ ♥ and you can't go wrong

And if a 🎬 isn't ready don't drop it yet

Keep at that 💪 💪 💪 until it's GREAT

OK???

I didn't know what to write back. That was A LOT of emojis he'd just laid on me. Finally, I wrote:

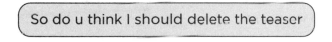

So do u think I should delete the teaser

He wrote back with a:

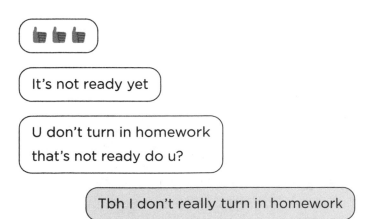

👍 👍 👍

It's not ready yet

U don't turn in homework that's not ready do u?

Tbh I don't really turn in homework

U should start champ!!!

School is IMPORTANT

OK I gotta go do laundry now

*Wuuuut?* Man, I couldn't believe that! I wrote back:

U DO LAUNDRY???

Then he wrote:

Heck yeah

How else u think I get my drawers clean???

 😂 😂 😂

Get back to bed champ! It's late where u r

Catch u later

There was no chance of me getting back to bed after that. I'd been DM'ing with Tevin Bart!

Plus, I'd just had twelve hours of sleep.

So what I did next was reread those DMs about ten times.

Especially the one where he said he believed in me. And I was a hundred-emoji talent.

Then I took his advice.

I deleted the teaser.

Now the only thing left on my channel was the original *Toothpick* movie.

Would folks who watched *The Helen Show* get mad when there wasn't a teaser like I'd promised? Would they subscribe anyway?

I know Tevin Bart had told me not to sweat the money emoji. But that was easy for him to say. Dude already HAD money emoji.

I didn't. So I couldn't help sweating it.

Would enough of those *Helen* watchers sign up that I could start monetizing? Show up Sierra and her dumb vlog channel?

And how bad did I clown myself on that show? When it aired, how big a fool was I gonna look?

I figured I'd find out soon enough.

## CHAPTER 23

# THE HELEN SHOW DROPS . . . ON MY HEAD

Dad got up early. Made us a big breakfast of pancakes and bacon with a whole lot of fresh fruit. I ate it wearing my fluffy *Helen Show* robe. Drank some orange juice out of that coffee mug, too.

Over breakfast, I showed Dad the DMs from Tevin Bart.

"Pretty solid of him to take the time," Dad said. "Gave you good advice."

"So you think it was a good idea to take down the teaser?" I asked.

Dad nodded. "I think so."

That got me mad. "Then why'd you tell me to put it up?"

"I don't know from teasers!" Dad said. "Plus, Tevin Bart don't have to live with you if you get mad and quit talking to him."

I couldn't argue that.

Going to school that day was weird. Word had gone 'round that Sierra and I were on *Helen*, so I was getting more of that mad-respect energy when I walked down the hall. Kids kept asking, "You really gonna be on *The Helen Show*?" And "What's it like?" And all of that.

But I didn't get any Elektro jolt from it this time. 'Cause down in the pit of my belly, I was afraid of how I'd look when the show dropped.

Plus, I was still dragging from those two nights of not enough sleep. I just wanted the day to be over so I could go home and check out the show. Then maybe take a nap.

*The Helen Show* comes on at 2:00. School ends at 2:55. My phone had been dead since lunch, 'cause I'd been checking my subscriber number all morning. It wasn't going up, but at least it had stopped going down.

After school, I ran to the bus. Soon as I got off it, I ran home. Plugged my phone in, and the first thing I saw when it restarted was a text from Aunt Janice. She watches *Helen* just about every day. So I'd been expecting her to chime in.

Here's what her text said:

> Oh baby u r just TOO MUCH 😂 😂 😂

What did THAT mean? Was it good or bad?

I got out Dad's laptop and went straight to the *Helen Show* website. They put up a clip of every segment after it airs.

I watched my whole segment.

And OH, MAN.

It was bad news from the get-go.

I came out looking like a deer in the headlights. Just about fell over that table. Whole crowd laughed at me.

Then I just sat in the chair looking stupid while Sierra charmed Helen and everybody else.

When I finally opened my mouth, it got even worse. I was a babbling fool!

Helen was goofing on me! Whole crowd was laughing at me!

Tevin Bart came on and took the Sierra lovefest to a whole other level. Every one of those props he gave the movie? They were all for stuff SHE did!

Girl soaked it up like a diva. Started hyping her channel, all full of herself.

Then I got that zinger in about her getting sued.

FINALLY! Something was going my way!

But then I started hyping my own channel. Looked just as full of myself as Sierra did.

Then came the primo donut stuff.

And there was no doubt about it.

I looked a grade A, five-star, self-clowning FOOL. Jumping out of my seat to tell the world what a jerk I was!

I couldn't even watch to the end. Had to turn it off and shut the laptop.

Then I didn't know WHAT to do.

I felt TERRIBLE!

Like I wanted to crawl out of my skin!

Go hide under a rock!

It was like all that Elektro attention energy I'd been soaking up the past few days was getting sucked right back out of me in reverse. And then some. Like I was Negative Elektro!

I texted Dad. But he was busy on his shift. So he couldn't text back.

Didn't know who else to text. I couldn't think of a single person I could talk to who wouldn't make me feel even worse.

For a minute, I wished my mama was still around.

But then I got to thinking it was better she wasn't. 'Cause I wouldn't have wanted her to see that.

I popped open the laptop again. By that point, checking my MeTube numbers was like breathing. As long as I had internet, I couldn't go more than two minutes without looking at them.

That's when I realized *Toothpick Fights the Doom!* was blowing up all over again.

*2,184,348.*

*2,193,041.*

*3,000,284 . . .*

My subscriber number was in overdrive, too!

*698.*

*702 . . .*

At that rate, I'd monetize by dinnertime!

Or maybe not. It was math. I couldn't do it.

*I gotta start paying attention in that class!* That's what I was thinking.

As for those numbers blowing up again, I didn't know WHAT to think.

If I clowned myself in front of the whole world . . . but then I made actual money from it?

That'd be like . . . the worst best thing that ever happened to me.

Or the best worst thing. The beworstest thing!

But maybe . . .

Well, maybe it'd be okay.

When I thought about it, I wasn't sure if I knew anybody who watched *The Helen Show* on the regular except Aunt Janice.

And if the only people who saw me act a fool were a bunch of folks I'd never even met . . . and they watched the *Toothpick* movie . . . and I got PAID for those clicks?

Well, that'd be just fine! Right?

*It's all good*, I said to myself. *Nobody watches that dumb show anyway.*

## CHAPTER 24

# EVERYBODY WATCHES THAT DUMB SHOW!

If you want to know how many people watch a TV show? Go on it and show your butt. Then count how many people tell you about it.

If it's *The Helen Show*? That number's gonna be about five people short of EVERYBODY ON EARTH!

I was getting texts that night from numbers I didn't even know! All of them goofing on me!

I got so many ClickChat DMs, I had to switch my account to private!

But by the time Dad came home from work that night? I ALSO had 1,010 subscribers. And it was still going up by the minute.

## Toothpick_Superhero

1,018 subscribers

After dinner, Dad sat with me at the laptop and filled out all the stuff we had to send to MeTube to get me monetized. Got it done in record time. By the next morning, there were ads playing at the front and back of the movie.

So I was getting paid! I just didn't know how much yet.

But no matter how much it was, I'll tell you this: it wasn't enough to make up for how bad I felt getting clowned like that.

School the next day was a nightmare. Remember those kids I barely knew, coming up to me all excited? Wanting me to introduce them to Tevin Bart?

Well, they were still coming up to me. But only so they could laugh in my face.

It was the opposite of respect. I was full-on Negative Elektro! Getting the life drained out of me by every dumb kid who flapped their gums in my direction.

The clowning was so bad, it gave me a bellyache. Had to go to the nurse's office.

Nurse just made things worse. 'Cause all SHE wanted to know was what Helen was really like in person.

I said, "Shiny." That's all I could remember of Helen.

I hid out in the nurse's office the whole rest of the day. Didn't leave until the Afternoon Adventures bell had rung. I was hoping by then it was late enough that I could sprint to the bus stop and get home before anybody else had a chance to laugh at me.

But when I hit the sidewalk, I ran straight into Tyrell and his crew.

"What's the hurry, Little Man?" he roared. "You off to tear it up on another talk show?"

"Bet he's off to buy himself some PRIMO DONUTS!" yelled Sly.

Then they all had a good laugh. I was so over it by then, I clapped back. Didn't even care if they beat me down for it.

"Since when do y'all watch *The Helen Show*?" I asked them. "What you do? Sit around the TV every afternoon like a bunch of gossipy grannies?"

They just laughed. "I ain't even seen the TV show," Tyrell told me. "But you're blowing up Flitter! A trending meme! Show him, Naz."

Naz got his phone out. Did some thumb punching. Then held out the phone to show me a flit. There was a GIF of me crowing on *The Helen Show*. My eyes bugging out. My mouth so big, I looked like one of those tropical snakes that swallows a whole goat in one bite.

Oh, man! I was the laughingstock of the whole internet!

I must've looked so busted down, even Tyrell felt sorry for me.

"Got some hard times ahead of you, Little Man," he said. "Once you're a Flitter meme? There's no coming back from that. You marked for life."

Then he gave it a shoulder shrug, like me being marked for life was no big deal. "You seen Sierra around?"

"No," I said. "Why you ask?"

"I gotta talk business with that girl," he told me. "She's blowing up! But not like you. She's doing it in a GOOD way."

Naz piped up again. "You seen that GIF of Sierra givin' you side-eye? That's a meme now, too! All over Flitter! It's SAVAGE."

The thought of Sierra getting the good kind of famous while I was getting the bad kind? That was just about the last straw. When I heard that, I felt two inches tall.

"That's great, Naz," I told him. "Can't wait to see it. Must be real special."

Tyrell frowned. Then he put his hand on my shoulder. Almost like a big brother would. "You okay, Little Man?" he asked me. "Never seen you this sad. Are you taking care of your mental health?"

"I don't even know, man," I told him. "It's been a week. Y'all threw garbage cans at me for half an hour the other day!"

"That was pretty cold," Tyrell admitted.

Double D's eyebrows bunched up like he was thinking it over. "We probably shouldn't have done that," he said.

"It was funny at the time," Sly pointed out.

Naz nodded. "Yeah. But I could see how Little Man might've taken it wrong."

Tyrell gave me a pat on the back. "Don't you worry, Little Man," he told me. "We won't throw any more garbage cans at you. Might want to get yourself home and take a nap now. You looking pretty ragged." He turned away. "C'mon, y'all! Let's find Sierra. Have ourselves that business talk."

The four of them walked off. And I ain't gonna lie, part of me was hoping the business talk might end with Sierra getting turned upside down and shaken out like Tyrell shook me.

But it didn't seem like it was going to go down that way.

Tyrell wanting to talk business with Sierra got me wondering what was up with her MeTube channel. So when I got back home, I checked it out.

First, I looked at my own channel. 'Cause that was always my first stop.

My numbers were solid. Almost five million views on the movie! Over two thousand subscribers!

Got me feeling pretty cocky.

But then I clicked over to the *Sierra Cinematic Universe.*

The last time I'd checked, her page views were just sad. But being on *The Helen Show* had changed all that.

Part one of *Phone Zombies* had three million views already!

And her first vlog was up. Less than a day old. Called "BEHIND THE SCENES AT THE HELEN SHOW: PART ONE!"

It had almost half a million views!

I played it. Started out with Jazmin showing up at Sierra's place before sunrise with a makeup kit. Doing Sierra's face. Every few seconds, the video cut to a close-up of Sierra, cracking some joke about what was happening.

Her whole fake-TV-host personality was annoying. But I had to admit—for what it was, that vlog wasn't bad. The girl was funny. And her editing game was tight.

But then came the part where Sierra and her mom got in the limo. The one I barfed in.

And . . . OH, MAN.

I can't even tell you what I watched, it made me so mad!

She used the footage of me! Like she said she wouldn't!

Put some kind of effect on it so my body was all blurred over. Looked like a fuzzy blob in the middle of the shot. And whenever I talked, she bleeped over it.

But it was OBVIOUS it was me!

Then she kept cutting in to make jokes about how I wouldn't let her use the footage!

She was shaming me!

Like I hadn't gotten enough of that already!

Got me so twisted up, I almost started to cry.

I texted her:

TAKE THAT VLOG DOWN!!!

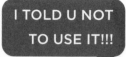

> I TOLD U NOT TO USE IT!!!

> TAKE IT DOWN OR I WILL SUE U!!!

A minute later, she texted me back:

> OK

> I'll take it down

> But then u have to take down the Toothpick movie

> Cuz I am all over that. And u never got a release from me

> So I will sue u too

The girl had me there. Mad as I was, there was nothing I could do but punch pillows and yell at the ceiling.

So that's what I did. Went Wolf Boy wild all over the living room. When I finally came back to my phone, there was one more text from Sierra:

Seeing that made me feel better.

*At least I'm making money and she ain't. Bet she's jealous.*

That's what I was thinking.

But then I checked her subscriber number.

## The_Sierra_Cinematic_Universe

1,201 subscribers

When I saw she'd monetized too, I went right back to feeling bad.

And I didn't stop for a good long time.

# CHAPTER 25

# SUPER SOUR SATURDAY

By the end of the next week, I was not in a good place mentally.

Going to school was just brutal. I'd walk down the hall, and out of nowhere, somebody'd yell, "PRIMO DONUT!" Then everybody'd crack up. Like me not knowing Italian was the funniest thing ever.

It wasn't just school, either. I got on the bus one morning, and this lady two seats down kept staring at me. After a couple stops, she leaned over and said, "Excuse me— were you just on *The Helen Show*?"

I said, "Nope. Wasn't me. Must've been some other dude."

She gave me a big old grin. Said, "Well, you should thank your lucky stars. 'Cause the boy who was on it? MERCY!"

Then she cackled like a witch.

That kind of stuff happened so often that after a while, I quit leaving the house unless I had to. Just stayed inside and sat on the couch, staring at my MeTube numbers.

Did a lot of staring at Sierra's numbers, too. She was

putting out new vids every other day. Pretty soon, she had almost as many subscribers as I did!

She was doing collabs with the other kids, too. Stuff like "How to Look Fierce with Jazmin Stylez!" and "Jamming with Amari!" Even did one called "Khalid's Stop-Motion Extravaganza."

They were all hyping their own channels now. Promoting them like they were a group. Called themselves the Killer Media Crew. Sierra texted me to ask if I wanted to be part of it.

I didn't even text back. I was done with that girl FOREVER.

But freezing out Sierra didn't make me feel better.

Nothing could make me feel better for a while there. I was like some nasty mash-up of Negative Elektro, plus a side of Swamp Zombie and a little dash of Wolf Boy.

Like I was Swamp Wolf Zombie Elektro Burnout Boy.

The next Saturday afternoon, J.R. called me up. It was two weeks after I'd first gone viral. He wanted to play some GameBox. I wasn't doing anything except lying on the couch, googling stuff like "How much do you make for a million MeTube views?" So I said okay.

When I opened the door for him, he gave me a funny look.

"You going swimming or something?"

I was in my *Helen Show* bathrobe. By then, it was pretty much all I wore around the house.

"No, man. I just like to be comfortable."

"Did you steal that from the show?"

"No! They gave it to me! Gave me a coffee mug, too."

"You gonna start drinking coffee?"

"I'm thinking about it."

We sat down on the couch. Started shooting zombies.

But I just wasn't feeling it. Put the controller down so I could check my numbers.

"I'm fixin' to hit seven million views tonight," I told J.R.

"Good for you," he said. "How 'bout you help me clear this level?"

"In a minute," I said. "Just gotta check something else."

I clicked over to the *Sierra Stupid Cinematic Universe.*

"Dang!" I said to J.R. "Part one of *Phone Zombies* just passed six million."

"That's cool," he said. His voice was all flat. Should've tipped me off something was wrong.

"My movie's better," I told him. "It's just that her stuff is shorter. So more people watch it. But part two only got two million hits so far! Her audience is slipping! Bet I end up making more money than she does."

J.R. put down his controller and blew up at me. "Man, will you shut up about your money?"

"I'm just saying!"

"What makes you think I want to hear it?"

That got me mad. "Ain't you my friend? Don't you want to know what's up with me?"

"I KNOW what's up with you!" he yelled. "It's all you talk about! And I'm sick of it! Struttin' around like a rooster—"

"STRUTTIN' AROUND?" I yelled. "Man, I can't even leave the house! You know how bad it feels when the whole world's goofin' on you?"

"Least they're talking about you!" he said. "You're lucky! But you keep acting like you're UN-lucky! Feeling sorry for yourself while you shove your money in my face!"

"I don't even HAVE money yet!" It was true. I had no idea when MeTube might start paying out.

But that didn't matter to J.R. He got up off the couch.

"Where you going?" I asked him.

"Anywhere but here," he told me.

"Some friend YOU are!" I yelled.

Then I heard the door slam.

*He's just jealous.* That's what I told myself.

Then Dad came in the room. I'd forgotten he was even home. It was his day off, and he'd been taking a nap in his bedroom.

I didn't like the way he was looking at me. Like I'd done something wrong.

"What?" I said.

"You going to apologize to J.R. now? Or later? 'Cause one way or another, it's got to happen."

"What did I even do?"

"Made him feel small."

"He made ME feel small!"

"Son, I heard the whole thing. You were in the wrong."

I couldn't believe it. Even my dad was against me!

There was a nasty lump building up in my throat. Like I might cry.

"Why you taking his side?" I yelled. "Why can't you take MY side?"

"Because you're WRONG," Dad told me again. "All this MeTube nonsense broke your brain, son. It's turning you into somebody I don't much like. What would your mama say if she saw you carrying on this way?"

Hearing that was just too much. I started to cry. Once I started, I couldn't stop. I don't know where all the emotion was coming from. But I was sobbing so hard, my whole body shook.

I think it freaked Dad out a little. He sat down next to me on the couch and wrapped me in a hug. "It's okay," he told me. "I love you. And I've always got your back. But that doesn't mean I can't tell you when you're wrong."

"You don't know how bad it feels," I told him. "The whole world hates me!"

"That's not even close to true," he said. "Nobody hates you, Marcus. They're just goofing on you a little. And I know it feels bad. But it'll pass."

"It's never gonna pass, Dad! I'm a MEME! There's no coming back from that!"

Dad just chuckled. "I'm not even clear on what that means," he told me. "But it's definitely wrong." Then he gave me a smile. "Hey, you know what I bet would cheer you up? Choköbjär!"

"You gotta go to Europe for those!" I told him.

"Do you now?" Dad got up, went to the kitchen. Came back with a handful of mini Choköbjärs.

"Where'd you get those?" I asked him.

"Took them home from *The Helen Show*," he said. While I was tearing into them, Dad picked up his laptop from the couch. He unplugged my phone from the charger and took that, too. Headed into his bedroom with them.

I started feeling panicky. "Where you taking those?"

He didn't answer. But when he came back a few seconds later, he was empty-handed.

"You're going to give them back, right?"

"I will in a bit," he told me. "But you need a break from all that nonsense. How about you and me take a walk downtown? Get some burgers for dinner and catch a movie?"

That's what we did. I changed out of my *Helen* robe and into normal clothes. Then we left the house. Walked enough miles to get good and hungry. Chowed down at a burger joint. Bought ourselves a pair of tickets to the seven o'clock showing of a new monster movie.

Dad was right—I DID need a break from all that nonsense. By the time we settled into our seats in the theater, I was feeling better than I had all week.

Then Dad reached in his jacket pocket. Pulled out another handful of mini Choköbjärs.

"You want some dessert?" he asked.

"Dang, Dad! How many of those did you take?"

"That's between me and the Lord, son." He gave me a wink. I couldn't help smiling back.

The monster movie was pretty bad. But it was a fun kind of bad. We took the bus home. By the time we got back, I was ready to conk out.

"Can I have my phone back?" I asked Dad.

"What for?"

Truth was, I wanted to check my numbers. But I knew Dad wouldn't want to hear that.

"Just want to see if anybody texted me," I told him.

He went in his bedroom. Came back a couple seconds later.

"You're all good. No new texts."

"Can I have my phone back anyway?"

"Why don't you let it be for a while?" he asked.

"Can I have the laptop, then?"

"What for?"

"Just to look at stuff."

"Like those numbers? So you can stare at them till you make yourself miserable again?"

"Dad! I gotta check my numbers!"

"Why?"

"Because!"

"Because why? You're too hung up on them, son. Those numbers aren't you. They're just numbers. And they're going to do what they do whether you look at them or not."

"Can I have my electronics back tomorrow?"

He frowned. "I think you might need more time off than that."

I was starting to get panicky again. "You can't just take my internet away! I'm on vacation!"

It was true. We had a break coming up. I was looking at a full week of no school!

"Great!" said Dad. "How about you take a vacation from the internet, too?"

"DAD! YOU CAN'T DO THAT!" I was freaking out. My heart was pounding!

Dad just nodded his head, slow and sad. "See that reaction there? That's why I HAVE to do it."

## CHAPTER 26

# DIGITAL DETOX

I gotta say: that first day without internet? It was HARD. I had the itch! Kept wanting to check those numbers every five minutes!

But I couldn't. Didn't matter how much I begged him. Dad cut off all my electronics except GameBox. Which he said I could only play if I was with J.R. And if I was going to call up J.R. to do some gaming, first I had to apologize to him for being a jerk.

So I did. J.R. was cool with it. And he was happy to hang out as long as I didn't talk about my page views or my subscriber numbers. Which was annoying. Because it meant I couldn't borrow HIS phone to look at my numbers.

But we had a good time anyway. We smashed thumbs for a few hours. Then we walked over to Monster Comics. Neither one of us had money to buy anything. But it was fun just looking. I hadn't been to the comics store in weeks. Just looking at the new covers got me inspired to do some drawing of my own.

After I got home, I sat down to make something new. Hadn't drawn anything since I'd sketched out that Hatebot 3000 a couple weeks back. I wasn't feeling the Hatebot anymore. Had an idea for a whole other kind of villain.

It was the worst kind of all: a traitor! Starts out seeming like a hero. An ally for Toothpick. He gets to trusting they can work together to fight crime.

Then, BAM! She betrays him!

New villain was named Secret Snake. It was this tall lady with long braids in her hair that turn into cobras!

I'll tell you what: it's not easy to draw a supervillain with a head full of snakes. Those first few sketches took forever to get right.

It was fine, though. With Dad taking my internet away, I had nothing but time.

When he came home for dinner, I showed him my
Secret Snake sketches.

"That's dope, Marcus!"

"It is, right?"

"For sure! You're on to something!" The way Dad was
smiling, I could tell he wasn't just saying that to be nice.
"Keep going, son!"

"I'm going to make a whole comic this week, Dad!
Twenty pages! Maybe more!"

"Good on you! Can't wait to see it!"

"Yeah!" I said. "So I'll mostly be doing that the whole
vacation. But, y'know, I gotta take breaks. Give my hand

a rest. So while I'm resting, I was thinking maybe I could get my phone back—"

When he heard the word "phone," Dad busted up laughing. Didn't even let me finish the sentence.

"Oh, heck, no, son! Save your breath."

That night before I went to sleep, I reread some old *Justice Team* comics. They gave me some more ideas for my story.

I decided Secret Snake wouldn't just betray Toothpick— she'd spread lies about him, too! That'd turn a bunch of the other superheroes against him.

There were four of them: Beautygirl, Beatbox, Brains, and the Brick. They'd all gang up on Toothpick, try to run him out of Center City!

I got so into the story, I even had dreams about it. Woke up in the morning with so many ideas, I could barely get them all down on paper! That whole week, I'd work on them every morning until J.R. showed up to do some gaming. We'd play for a bit. Then he'd leave to go shoot hoops, and I'd get back to work on my comic.

Every night when Dad came home, I'd show him what I'd done. He was into it!

J.R. was, too! They were both like, "Man, this is your best Toothpick yet!"

I had to agree. I was in the zone. By the end of that week, I had a dozen pages. It was slower going than I'd thought, on account of how much detail I was putting into some of the panels. And how long it took to draw all those stupid snakes on the villain's head.

But those finished pages looked dope! They were so good, I got to thinking I might even be able to take this one all the way.

Sell it to Capital Comics!

I mean, why not? If I could go viral with a movie, why couldn't I hit it big with a comic, too?

Truth is, that's all I ever wanted—to be a real comic book artist! The kind whose stuff gets sold on the racks down at Monster. That was my dream. Way before I ever got into all that movie nonsense.

It wasn't like I grew up wanting to make movies. That was Sierra's dream. I just caught the bug from her.

And don't get me wrong: I LIKED making that *Toothpick* movie.

But I didn't LOVE movies. Not like I love comics. And not like I love drawing.

Even so . . .

As I thought about it, lying in bed one night toward the end of the week . . . the one thing I DID like better about movies was that I didn't have to do it alone.

Drawing comics—especially when you hit a rough patch, with the story or the way you're trying to draw one of the characters—well, it can get lonely.

When you're making a movie, there's always somebody

by your side. If you've got a problem, you can talk it over with them. Share ideas.

And when the movie's all done, it's not just yours. It's everybody's! And as good as it feels to make something all by yourself? It feels even better when you're on a team.

There was a downside, too. I sure didn't miss all those arguments I used to get into with Sierra. But when the whole thing was clicking, and we were making some magic together? You couldn't beat that.

The next day, I got to thinking about it some more. And I realized there was one other thing that movies had over comics: the audience.

It could be HUGE! What was *Toothpick Fights the Doom!* up to by now? Eight or nine million views, maybe? It was seven million when Dad took my phone away.

That was just mind-blowing!

Heck, I bet the biggest comic book artist in the world didn't get nine million eyes on their comic!

At least, not until somebody made it into a movie.

But maybe it was a good thing my new comic wouldn't get all those eyes on it. 'Cause at the end of the day, getting all that attention bit me HARD in the butt. Didn't feel good at all.

And yeah, a comic book artist might not get invited on a talk show. But that also meant a talk show couldn't ruin their life by turning them into an internet meme!

Although, truth was ... maybe *The Helen Show* hadn't

totally ruined my life. As long as I wasn't online or at school, or getting recognized by strangers on the bus, it didn't really register at all.

By Friday night of that vacation week, I'd almost stopped even thinking about it.

And I was riding high on that creative buzz from the new comic I was making.

After dinner Friday night, Dad reread every single page. Then he gave me a big old smile.

"I'm proud of you, boy. This is some dope work! You ACCOMPLISHED something this week! Aren't you glad I took those electronics away? Gave you the space to do this, instead of lying on the couch, staring at your numbers?"

"If I say yes, will you give back my phone?" I asked.

"Do you really want it back?" He nodded at the pages. "This comic's not done yet. I still don't know how Toothpick's going to get out of this mess!"

"You want me to tell you how it ends?"

"No! I want you to DRAW it!"

"Of course I'm going to draw it, Dad! I'm an artist! That's what I do!"

"So why do you need your phone back?"

"So I can live in the world again! Like every other kid I know."

Dad thought it over. Then he nodded. "That's fair. But you gotta promise me you're not going to get back on that tiger. Get all obsessed with looking at those numbers again."

"I promise, Dad! I won't check them more than once a day."

"Once a WEEK," he said. "At most!"

"Okay! Once a week!"

"Promise?"

"Yes!"

"All right, then."

Dad went to his bedroom. Fetched my phone from wherever he'd hidden it. Handed it back to me. I had a whole mess of new texts. Most of them were nonsense.

But then there were the ones from Sierra.

Hey dude. Can we talk?

I'm sorry how
everything went down.

I know I did you wrong.
And I want to make it right

*How 'bout that?* I thought to myself. *The chickens are coming home to roost.*

I decided not to text her back at all. Just freeze that girl out.

Forever! Never speak to her again in my life!

I lasted about five minutes. Then I texted her back.

## CHAPTER 27

# A TALK IN THE PARK

Sierra wanted to talk in person. So we met up first thing Saturday morning on a bench at this little park about halfway between her place and mine. Seemed like good neutral territory for a peace conference.

She said she was sorry for everything. Especially calling me a prima donna on *Helen*.

"Why'd you diss me like that?" I asked her.

"Because you dissed me first," she said. "Hurt my feelings."

"I hurt YOUR feelings?"

"Yes! You called my channel 'a bunch of dumb vlogs.' And I hadn't even posted any yet! And you said I didn't know from good! You started the whole thing, Marcus."

"No, I didn't!"

"Yes, you did! Go back and watch the tape! You hit me first! All I did was fight back."

"Huh."

I had to think about that for a bit. The whole time I'd been mad at Sierra, I'd never once thought any of it was my fault.

Was it?

"Did I really start the whole thing?" I asked her.

"Yes!"

"Oh, man . . . ! Well, I guess I'm sorry, too." Then I thought of something. "But wait!"

"What?"

"Why'd you post that vlog of me barfing in the limo? When I said you couldn't?"

"I'm sorry for that, too," she said. "But I blurred out your face and your voice. That makes it legal. And how could I NOT use it? It was hilarious! That clip was gold!"

"You gonna share that gold with me? Now that you monetized?"

"If I do, are we good?" she asked.

I thought it over.

Truth was, if I'd kinda started that whole fight on *Helen* . . . maybe I shouldn't be so mad. And after a week of not being online, I already wasn't half as mad as I had been.

Plus, me barfing in that limo WAS pretty funny. If I were her, I probably would've posted it, too.

"I guess we'd be good," I finally said.

"So if we're gooooood . . ." she said in her schoolteacher voice.

That's when I realized she didn't just come to apologize. This girl wanted something.

"Here it comes," I said.

She smiled like I'd busted her. "I was just wondering . . . if I write a sequel to *Phone Zombies* . . . would you come back and play Puffer again?"

"You gonna make another movie? I thought you were all vlogs all the time now."

She huffed out a big sigh. "Truth is . . . I just like making movies better. I don't want to be ME all the time. I want to play characters! And that vlog stuff is a lot harder than it looks. You know how many hours I gotta spend editing just to make one video? I been up half the night every day this week!"

"I watched that *Tall Girl Troubles* vlog you just dropped," I told her.

"Yeah? What'd you think? Real talk."

"Real talk?" I gave her a shoulder shrug. "Wasn't feeling it."

She didn't like hearing that. But she'd asked for the truth!

"Maybe you just couldn't identify," she said. "On account of not being a tall girl."

I shrugged. "I guess not. But it wasn't your best work. The behind-the-scenes stuff was better. Even though you sold me out. And some of those collabs with the other kids were good, too."

Sierra nodded. "I gotta rethink that whole *Tall Girl* concept. Maybe just ditch the whole thing. But what do you say to a *Phone Zombies* sequel? Will you do it with me? The rest of the KMC's all in."

"The KMC?" I'd forgotten what that even was.

"The Killer Media Crew! Jazmin, Amari, Khalid, Tyrell—"

"Now, hang on a sec," I said. "Tyrell's got a MeTube channel now?"

Sierra's eyes lit up. "You haven't seen *Tyrell's Treats*?"

"Tyrell's WHAT?"

"*Tyrell's Treats*! It's a baking channel! And the dude is killing it! Did you know he could bake?"

My eyebrows must've gone up near the top of my skull when I heard that. "No, I did not. He never mentioned it while he was turning me upside down and throwing garbage cans at me."

"Dude's got serious kitchen skills," Sierra said. "Makes a sticky bun that melts in your mouth. I helped him shoot the vlog for it. He's got ten thousand views already! Fixin' to drop his monkey bread episode next week."

"Dang!" I said. "That's some wild stuff."

"Not only that," Sierra went on, "he's signed on to play the villain in the next *Phone Zombies*. Be the Phone King! Ruler of the zombie horde! It's gonna be fire. Especially if you come back and play Puffer. What do you say?"

I'm not gonna lie: what Sierra was saying sounded pretty good. We had a lot of fun making that first *Phone Zombies* movie. And when we screened it at the Fall Arts Showcase, I got mad laughs from the crowd. The GOOD kind of laughs.

But I was only just getting back to a good mental place. And I didn't want to mess it up by showing my butt on the internet again.

"I dunno," I told her. "I got my own thing going right now."

"What's that?"

"Making a new comic."

"Is it a Toothpick?" she asked.

I nodded. "Got a brand-new villain. Called Secret Snake. She's this tall, nasty lady with braids on her head that turn into snakes."

"Oh, really?" Sierra twirled one of her braids around her finger. "That based on anybody I know?"

"Course not! It's just made up. Unless you know any snakes."

She gave me a smirk. "You gonna make a movie out of it?"

That was a very good question. And the truth was . . . I'd already had some thoughts about turning it into a movie.

But if I did, I couldn't do it alone.

And I wasn't sure if I wanted to get back into that whole mess.

"The thing is," I said, "that last time didn't work out so good for me."

She looked at me like I was out of my mind. "Didn't work out so good? You got millions of views! You MONETIZED! And it made you FAMOUS!"

"But I got BAD famous!" I told her.

"No, you didn't! You're GOOD famous."

"Girl, are you out of your mind? Whole world's out there calling me a primo donut!"

Sierra laughed. "Dude! That is AWESOME. You got your own catchphrase!"

"Catchphrase for being a fool!"

"Catchphrase for being FUNNY!" She shook her head, smiling from ear to ear. "Marcus, you made people laugh! That's a valuable thing! All you gotta do is OWN it. Be proud! Like you're in on the joke. You know what I'D do?"

"What?"

"I'd rename your whole channel *Primo Donuts*. That's a dope brand! It's so dope, you'd better take it quick, before somebody else does."

"It's humiliating! Everybody's laughing at me!"

"Not necessarily. They're just laughing. All you gotta do is laugh WITH them. Quit taking yourself so serious! Have some fun with it. Fact is, dude: you got a big mouth. Runs about twice the speed of your brain. And you're always flying off the handle. But it can be hilarious! And if you just own it? I'm telling you, whatever YOU think of yourself? That's what other people will think of you, too."

I rolled my eyes at that.

"It's true! Next time somebody calls you a primo donut, lean into it! Say, 'That's right, son! I'm THE primo donut!' Hype yourself like a rapper! Or a pro wrestler. I'll bet you anything you'll get respect for it. You're already a meme!"

"I know! I'm marked for life!"

"In a good way! Just embrace it, and folks will embrace you, too. I guarantee it. You got a prime opportunity here. You know how many comics would kill for that kind of free publicity?"

I'd never thought about the situation that way. It was a pretty wild idea. Couldn't tell if Sierra was being straight with me. Or just trying to gas me up so I'd say yes to being in her movie.

"So what do you say?" Sierra asked again. "If you sign on to *Phone Zombies 2*? After we shoot it, I'll do *Toothpick Fights the Snake Hair Lady* with you. Or whatever else you want."

"I just don't know if I even want to make movies anymore," I said.

Sierra gave me a snort. Rolled her eyes. "Yeah, you do. You *know* you do! Come on, dude! Let's make some dope stuff together. Blow people's minds! Get rich and famous!"

"I gotta think it over," I said.

It was true. What she'd just dropped on me was A LOT. Made my head spin! I needed to go someplace quiet. Get my mind straightened out enough to think it all through.

Maybe get some good advice, too. From somebody who had my back no matter what.

I knew just the place for that.

## CHAPTER 28

# WHAT REALLY MATTERS

Usually when I visit Mama's grave, I go with Dad. But this time, I went alone. Wanted to have a private talk with Mama. Just the two of us.

I would've brought flowers, but I didn't have any money for them.

So instead, I brought her a mini Choköbjär from Dad's stash. Mama loved chocolate just as much as she loved to laugh. I unwrapped it for easier eating. Laid it on the base of her gravestone, straight down from the second "A" in ANGELA JENKINS.

Then I sat down on the grass in front of the stone and tried to focus my thoughts on her.

*Hey there, Mama. Hope you're doing okay.*

An ant was walking across the base of the gravestone. Headed for that Choköbjär. I thought about flicking it away. But I didn't want to mess up the mood by killing some little ant that just wanted to eat a bit of chocolate. So I let it be. Closed my eyes so I could focus on my prayer to Mama.

*A lot's been happening lately. I don't know if they've got TV in heaven. But if you caught me on* The Helen Show, *all I can say is, I'm sorry if I shamed you by acting a fool.*

*Dad said it was fine. Said there's no such thing as bad publicity.*

*Sierra said so, too. Thinks I should be proud of it!*

*Make mouthing off my brand, I guess. Or something like that.*

*That seems messed up to me. I don't know.*

*I mean, if it's something to be proud of, how come it made me feel so bad?*

I opened my eyes. The ant had stopped in front of a little crumb of Choköbjär that had broken off from the rest. Started trying to pick it up. But there was no way. That crumb looked about ten times that ant's size.

I shut my eyes again. Went back to my prayer.

*I gotta say, Mama: All this attention I been getting? First for the movie, and then for the primo donut stuff? It's WEIRD.*

*It's kinda like electricity. You know how electricity can give you so much energy, you can power a whole city with it?*

*But at the same time, if you plug into it wrong, it'll blow you up?*

*That's what attention feels like. Especially on the internet.*

*And now Sierra wants me to make more movies with her. But I just don't know.*

*Maybe I should just keep to myself. Draw my comics.*

*Except it's kinda lonely. I like being with my friends. Working on stuff as a team.*

*But I just don't know—if I go down that road? And I get that attention again? Can I keep my head on straight next time? Not get all twisted up over numbers? And monetizing? And trolls in the comments? All that nonsense?*

*What do you think, Mama? If you got any ideas, give me a sign.*

I opened my eyes. Looked up at the sky. Some clouds were going by. I stared at them for a while, looking for a message in the shapes. If Mama was up in heaven, seemed like that'd be the best way to talk to me.

One of the clouds looked like a horse for a second. But then it didn't. And I didn't know what kind of message a horse would be, anyway.

Then I tried listening to the birds. Except none of them

were singing at that hour. Heard a few trucks rumbling in the distance, but that was about it.

I looked back at that ant on Mama's grave. He was still giving it all he had. But that crumb wouldn't budge.

Then I saw some movement out the corner of my eye.

It was more ants. A bunch of them. All marching across the base of that gravestone, headed straight for that first ant and the crumb that wouldn't budge.

When they got to the crumb, they all gathered around it, next to the first ant. Gave it a heave-ho. And before I knew it, I was watching those ants carry the crumb away.

*That's some teamwork*, I thought.

Then I shut my eyes and started praying again.

*Please, Mama. Just give me a little sign. Anything!*

My eyes sprang open. Those ants were marching off the stone, headed into the grass to feast on that Choköbjär crumb.

*Wait a minute. . . .*

*ARE THE ANTS IT?*

*Is that your message, Mama? That a bunch of ants together can do what one ant can't? And all they gotta do is be a team?*

*And that's what I should do? Go make movies with my friends?*

*Did you send me an ant message, Mama?*

I thought about that.

Then I decided it was just foolish.

*Man, that's not a sign! That's just some ants.*

I was still thinking about those ants when I got on the bus to go home.

It was pretty empty. Whole back half was just me and this teenage girl facing my way a few seats down.

After a stop or two, I realized she was giving me that LOOK.

Same kind of look that had kept me in the house for two weeks.

She leaned in toward me. I knew what was coming.

"Hey," she said. "Are you the primo donut kid?"

I almost told her no.

Then I remembered what Sierra had said. And I gave it a try.

"Heck, yeah, I'm the Primo Donut," I told her.

Her eyes got all wide. Couldn't tell if it was in a good way or a bad way.

I decided to push my luck. Raised my voice.

"I'm the triple-glazed, sugar-on-top, certified-fresh, ALWAYS-DELICIOUS PRIMO DONUT!"

She broke out in a smile so big it lit up the whole bus.

"That is SO AMAZING!" she squealed. "Can I get a selfie with you? My friends are gonna be so jelly!"

Me and that girl took selfies on her phone the whole

way home. My own phone was dead. But I gave her my number, and she texted the best ones to me. She was over the moon about it!

She was so hyped, I think if I'd asked that girl out before I got off the bus? She would've said yes. Even though she was about six inches taller than me.

*Dang!* I thought as I walked back to my house. *Maybe there ain't no such thing as bad publicity.*

*Maybe those ants really were trying to tell me something.*

I was still riding high when I got home. Dad was sitting at the kitchen table, going through some mail. He was looking pretty hyped.

"You get my text?" he asked me.

"Heck, no. My phone's been dead for hours."

"Might be time for a new phone, then."

"Don't even joke, Dad."

"What do you mean?"

"I been asking you to get me one forever! But you keep saying we can't afford it!"

Dad just smiled, real sly. "Well, I can't afford it," he said. "But YOU can."

"What you mean, Dad?"

He handed me an envelope from the stack of mail. Top of it was ripped open.

My heart just about stopped.

It was a letter from MeTube. And there was a check in it.

# CHAPTER 29

# A WHOLE LOT OF MATH

I REALLY need to start doing my math homework. That stuff is important!

Like, if you ever make some money? You're gonna need math to keep everything straight. For a couple reasons.

First reason is taxes.

Dad sat me down and explained it to me.

"The thing is, son, MeTube didn't take any tax money out of this check. But the government's gonna want their piece."

"It's my money. What's the government need it for?"

"Lots of stuff. Roads. The army."

"I gotta pay for THE ARMY?"

Dad just laughed. "It's a fact of life, son. Those planes they got? The high-tech ones? They ain't cheap."

"Aw, man! How much I gotta pay?"

"I don't know yet. Gotta look at the forms. Do the math."

"Is it a lot?"

"It's more than a little. Gonna have to set you up a bank account, too."

"How come?"

"To cash the check, for one thing. But you're also going to need some place to set that tax money aside until we send it in when you write out your tax returns."

"I gotta write TAX RETURNS?"

"Sure do! It's like homework the government gives you. Except if you do it wrong, you go to jail."

"WHAT?"

"Don't worry. They ain't going to send you to jail. But let's get those returns right just in case."

"Oh, man! How'd I get myself into this, Dad?"

Dad just shrugged. "It's the price of doing business."

"What if I don't WANT to do business?"

"It's too late for that, son. Made your bed back when you monetized. Now you gotta lie in it."

I couldn't believe it. The government was giving me homework! And taking my money!

But it wasn't all bad. After Dad eyeballed how much they were gonna take and subtracted it, there was still plenty left over.

Then I had to do ANOTHER kind of math.

Which was figuring out how much of that money to give my friends.

I'd already told them I'd share it. And they deserved it! This was *Toothpick* movie money. I couldn't have made that movie without them.

"So how do you want to divide it up?" Dad asked me.

It was a tough question. "Oh, man. I don't even know. Sierra gets the most, I guess—"

"More than you?"

I thought about it. "Actually, no. I should get the most. 'Cause I put the most work in. But Sierra gets the SECOND most. Sly, Naz, and Double D get the least since they just showed up for one day of filming. Everybody else gets somewhere in between."

I made up the list of everybody who worked on the movie. Dad helped me work out a formula where I guessed at the total number of hours each kid put in. Then I gave them a share based on how many hours they'd worked.

Figuring it all out took forever. It was just math on top of math! I should've showed it to my teacher for some extra credit!

The last number was the most important one. For me, anyway. After I subtracted the tax money and everybody else's shares, what was left over? That was MY money.

Turned out to be just enough to get me a new phone.

By the time Dad and I looked up the tax stuff, did all the math, went to the bank, filled out some forms, opened an account, deposited the check, waited for it to clear, took out the cash, went to the phone store, and bought me a phone, it was two weeks later.

The first thing I did after I got home and set up that brand-new phone was send a group text to all the other kids:

> Can we meet at Donut Shop at 3pm tomorrow?

AMARI

> U gonna buy us some primo donuts?

He was trying to wind me up. But when I saw that, I just smiled.

Then I texted back:

> Heck yeah I am

> Cuz I am THE PRIMO DONUT!!!

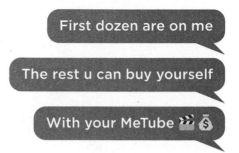

When they saw that?
My new phone LIT UP. They all went emoji-wild on me.
And it felt good.

# CHAPTER 30

# THE KILLER MEDIA CREW!

As dope as it was when I first got that MeTube money? It was even better to share it with my friends.

I'd split it all into envelopes with each kid's name on it. And when I gave them out? Man, I felt like I was Helen on that episode when she gave everybody in the audience a car!

Jazmin hugged me! Tyrell did, too! Jazmin's was a lot better. 'Cause it didn't squeeze all the air out of my lungs like Tyrell's did.

But he didn't hurt me on purpose. He was just excited.

Everybody was! Sly and Naz started whooping so loud, they almost got tossed out of the Donut Shop!

Eventually, we all settled down. Then we chowed on donuts and started making plans.

"How's your monster movie coming?" Sierra asked Khalid.

"Slow," he said. "That stop-motion takes forever. I'm thinking my next film should just be with real actors. Make some dope monster costumes for them."

"I can help you with the monster makeup," Jazmin told him. "Long as I'm not too busy painting *Phone Zombie* faces for the sequel. Where you at on that, Sierra?"

"I got a draft," she said. "But it's not good enough yet. Needs a rewrite. We might want to shoot the second Toothpick movie first."

"I ain't even close to ready with that," I told her. "Just finished drawing the comic. Now I gotta turn it into a screenplay."

"You want to get Toothpick on a collab?" Amari asked me. "Have him spit a verse on my next track?"

"No, man," I told him. "Toothpick doesn't do collabs. That's not his thing. He's a superhero."

They all looked at each other like, *Is this dude getting*

*a big head? Thinking he's all that?* But then I explained it to them.

"I got this whole OTHER character I want to roll out," I said. "Not a superhero at all. Just a normal kid. The Primo Donut! A trash-talking, gum-flapping, motormouthed fool! And he's down to collab all day."

Amari gave me a grin. "So the Primo Donut's gonna spit on a track?"

"You kidding? Man, you can't shut that dude up! Probably thinks he's a rap god even if he stinks."

"Does the Primo Donut need a makeover?" Jazmin asked me.

"Maybe," I said. "At least a haircut."

Jazmin liked the sound of that. "Ooooh! I haven't done a hair-for-boys episode in a minute. Gotta put that on the schedule."

Just then, Tyrell sat up straight and roared "AWWW, YES!" so loud we all jumped from fright.

"What you yelling about?" Double D asked him.

"I got a bomb idea!" Tyrell pointed across the table at me. "Little Man! That Primo Donut of yours gotta collab with me! On a special *Tyrell's Treats* DONUT EDITION!"

"Can you actually make a good donut?" Sierra asked him.

"I can make ANYTHING," Tyrell told her. "I'm the Kitchen King!"

"I thought you were my Zombie King," said Sierra.

"I'm all of it!" said Tyrell. "We gonna do it ALL, fam! Killer Media Crew gonna take over the world!"

We all had a good laugh at that.

But you know what?

Sitting around that table with my friends? Talking about all the dope projects we were going to create together?

I had a feeling Tyrell might be right.

And I couldn't wait to get started.

# Author's Note

What's up, book people???

Kevin Hart here: comedian, actor, producer, entrepreneur . . . and now, children's author.

It's not the usual career move. But when I was growing up in North Philly, there weren't a whole lot of kids' books I could see myself in. I want to do my part to put some new faces on your shelves.

Even more, I want to INSPIRE KIDS—especially the kids like me, who didn't have much growing up— to DREAM BIG and work their butts off to make those dreams come true.

When I was coming up, all I heard was NO. No, you can't. . . . No, you're not good enough. No, you don't have the right education or know the right people. . . .

Blah blah blah. I'm stubborn, so I turned those nos into fuel. Every time I heard one, it just made me work harder to prove wrong whoever said it.

But not every kid is like that. A lot of them hear NO and believe it. When they do, we ALL lose out. Because there's greatness in them! But if they quit before they even get started, it never has a chance to develop!

I wanted to create a story that'd help those kids believe in themselves by showing them somebody who's just like them, who draws his own road map and then follows it down a long, wild path to success.

The hero of *Marcus Makes a Movie* and *Marcus Makes It Big* is a lot like me when I was growing up. He doesn't have money or connections; he's not a great student or a star athlete. But he's got BIG DREAMS, and he's willing to put in the HARD WORK to make them come true. As Marcus and his partner-in-hustle, Sierra, try to turn his superhero-movie idea into an ACTUAL movie, they hit a ton of roadblocks. And they screw up a LOT. But these kids NEVER QUIT—and by the end of the first story, they've created something they're proud of.

And that's only the beginning of their journey. I'm cowriting this series of books with Geoff Rodkey, the dopest middle-grade author I know. We'll make EVERY kid who reads these books laugh, we'll make MOST of them cry (for real!)—and if we did our jobs right, we'll inspire some of them to GET OUT THERE AND HUSTLE after their dreams the same way I did.

Enjoy! It's a fun ride! And we're just getting started!

—KEVIN HART

**KEVIN HART** is an award-winning actor, a comedian, and a number one *New York Times* bestselling author. His films, including *Fatherhood, Jumanji, Captain Underpants*, and *The Secret Life of Pets*, have earned billions at the box office, and his stand-up comedy tours have sold out arenas and football stadiums, leading *Forbes* to name him the "king of comedy." His first middle-grade novel, *Marcus Makes a Movie*, was an instant *New York Times* bestseller and was published to great critical acclaim, with *Kirkus Reviews* praising it as "a charming read . . . that celebrates the gifts of authentic friendship" and *Publishers Weekly* calling it an "energetic love letter to the artistic process." In the laugh-out-loud sequel, *Marcus Makes It Big*, Kevin delivers a heartfelt message about the perils of sudden fame and the importance of sticking close to the friends and family who helped get you there.

Kevin is also an entrepreneur, a television producer, and the chairman of the Laugh Out Loud Network and CEO of HartBeat Productions. He lives in Los Angeles with his family. 📷 🐦

**GEOFF RODKEY** is the author of the best-selling Tapper Twins comedy series; the Chronicles of Egg adventure trilogy; *We're Not from Here*, an NPR and *Kirkus* Best Book of the Year; and *The Story Pirates Present: Stuck in the Stone Age*, a comic novel bundled with a how-to guide for kids who want to create stories of their own. His first novel for adults, *Lights Out in Lincolnwood*, was called "an irresistible story about a hapless family's efforts to survive the apocalypse" by *Publishers Weekly*. He is also the Emmy-nominated screenwriter of such films as *Daddy Day Care* and *RV*. Learn more at geoffrodkey.com, and follow Geoff on Twitter at @GeoffRodkey. 📷 🐦

**DAVID COOPER** is a multimedia artist and muralist, born and raised in Brooklyn, New York. His work has appeared on book covers, ad campaigns, and editorial publications, such as the *New York Times*, *Print* magazine, and *POZ* magazine. He has painted large-scale murals at Miami Art Basel, Brooklyn, and has been exhibited at the New York Society of Illustrators. Learn more about David's work at davidcooperart.com. 📷 🐦